# THE EGO
# HAS LANDED

# THE EGO HAS LANDED

## DAVID CHARTERS

E&T

First published 2009 by Elliott and Thompson Limited
27 John Street, London WC1N 2BX
www.eandtbooks.com

ISBN: 978-1-9040-2776-8

9 8 7 6 5 4 3 2 1

A CIP catalogue record for this book is available from
the British Library.

Printed in the UK by CPI Group

For 'Two Livers', wherever you are.

*Author's Note & Acknowledgements*

ONCE AGAIN I am indebted to a number of people who contributed to Dave Hart's further adventures. Lorne Forsyth, Jane Miller, Joanna Rice, Adam Shutkever, my oldest son Mark and my sister Margaret all contributed thoughts and comments, while my family put up with me while I was working on the latest instalment. But most of all I'm grateful to the investment bankers, hedge fund managers and others from the Square Mile who provide such extraordinary inspiration. And of course 'Two Livers', to whom this book is dedicated.

I'M DEAD.

I know I must be dead because I'm walking slowly up a long staircase in bare feet, wearing an old-fashioned nightgown, and I'm surrounded by puffy white clouds. Sitting or standing in the clouds are groups of beautiful young women, all dressed in long white gowns, all singing heavenly arias. I recognise Ilyana from Kiev, and Breathless Beth, and Fluffy and Thumper from the Pussycat Club, and there's a stunning redhead from Warsaw whose name I've forgotten. Choruses of heavenly hookers, all serenading me as I ascend the final steps to a pair of huge iron gates, and standing in front of them a very ancient man with a long beard, who is staring at a book on a lectern.

'Name?' He has a deep, gravelly voice, commanding and stern, the sort of voice that makes me worry in case he somehow knows my guilty secrets. All of them.

'H – Hart. Dave Hart.' My mouth is dry and it's an effort to get the words out. But at least I get a reaction as he looks up from the book.

'Dave Hart? Are you kidding? You're a fucking investment banker. Get out of here, you wanker!'

1

And suddenly a great wind is blasting through the railings of the gates and I'm tumbling, falling head over heels back down the stairs, and the girls have stopped singing and are all pointing at me and laughing, and I want to scream, need to scream, desperate to scream...

'Aaaaaaargh!'

I open my eyes. I'm lying in bed in a small room with white painted walls.

An institutional room. The bed is narrow and uncomfortable and is surrounded by medical equipment with wires running under the covers and dials and flashing lights. I know I'm in hospital, but as I scream the door of my room bursts open and a policewoman runs in followed by a nurse.

A policewoman? In a hospital? Oh, for fuck's sake. Now it's coming back to me. I rest my head back on the pillow and try not to laugh.

I'm an investment banker. And not just any investment banker. I'm Dave Hart. I run the investment banking operations of the Erste Frankfurter Grossbank – 'Grossbank' to its friends – which I've turned from Sleepy Hollow into one of the most happening places in the City of London in a little over twelve months.

And most of my friends are investment bankers too. I still can't recall exactly what I'm doing in hospital, but instinct takes over and I look at the policewoman and the nurse and grin.

My voice is croaky and it's an effort to speak. 'Don't tell me – Dan Harriman sent you.' Dan runs European equities at Hardman Stoney. He's what passes in investment banking circles for one of my closest friends –

which is to say that he's always there when he needs you. But now it's my turn and he's done me a favour.

'All right, get your kit off.' I nod to the policewoman. 'You first. I'll start with a blow-job.'

They look at each other, pretending to be surprised, and neither of them undoes so much as a button. I stare at them. They're not actually that pretty.

'Come on, I don't have all day.' Actually I do have all day. I'm aching all over, and can feel wires attached by sticking plaster at strategic points all over my body. What's going on?

The one who's dressed as a policewoman speaks first. 'Mister Hart – I'm Police Constable Hardy, attached to the Anti-Terrorist Squad.'

Now I'm impatient. You can take role-playing too far. 'Honey, cut the bullshit – just get your top off.' A thought is forming in my mind. I'm starting to blame that cheapskate Dan Harriman. Probably only paid for topless hand relief.

I close my eyes and sigh, half impatient, half exhausted, and am dimly aware of murmured voices, then something wet being rubbed on my bare arm, a sharp jab, and I drift off again.

\*       \*       \*

VOICES ARE talking in my head. One of them is female, deep and husky, a measured, unhurried voice, oozing sexuality, the sort of voice that could hypnotise you. She's talking to some kind of medic, a man, who seems nervous, almost intimidated by her.

'So how long till he wakes up?'

'Any time now. We're letting him rest. Sleep is a great cure. The body needs to heal itself, but so does the mind. What he went through must have been extraordinary.'

A hand rests on my shoulder and I can smell the unmistakable scent of Un Bois Vanille by Serge Lutens. 'He's tough. He can take a lot more than most of us.'

Before I can feel a surge of manly pride, the medic cuts in.

'Well, he certainly has. And our guess is that although he's been taking it for years, he really maxed out in the past twelve months. He's tested positive for opiates and cocaine – exceptionally high readings in both cases – his liver shows massive stress from alcohol abuse, and he seems to have been taking an enormous volume of drugs normally associated with penile erectile dysfunction.'

Penile erectile dysfunction? Me? Who does this guy think he is? Let him try shagging four hookers a night when he's high on coke and plastered with cocktails and champagne. That's it. I've had enough. My eyes pop open and I struggle to sit up in bed.

Standing next to me, wearing a pale grey Donna Karan trouser suit with a pashmina and huge diamond earrings, probably by Graff, is a vision of blonde loveliness. No, she's not a hooker, though she could earn a fortune if she chose to be – film stars, Presidents and tycoons would sell their souls for an hour of her company. And Dan Harriman definitely didn't send her. A woman this beautiful surely shouldn't have a brain as well, but Laura 'Two Livers' MacKay is an investment banker, one of the most dedicated, focussed, over-achieving storm troopers in the Square Mile. We call her Two Livers because she

4

has a biological advantage over the rest of us: she can drink for England, and frequently has done, giving her an advantage that mere intellect could never compete with. In fact, she's not just any banker, she's my number two running all corporate business at Grossbank, and suddenly a whole flood of memories return.

She sees my eyes open and leans close, so that I can feel her breath on my cheek.

'Hi boss. You okay?' I love it when a woman calls me boss. Especially a beautiful one.

She's got a sexy half smile on her face. It's the sort of wicked, 'come to bed' look that makes me want to tear the covers off, pull the wires off my body and… but instead I smile weakly and a pounding takes over in my head.

'Boss – you're not in great shape.'

'Wh – what do you mean?'

'There was a bomb under your car.'

I lie back and close my eyes. I remember. I'd just had a phone call from the love of my life, Sally 'Perfectly White Panties' Mills, mother of Toby, Jasper and Monty and wife of Trevor the underachieving teacher, a woman who can't be bought, who comes from a planet in a different galaxy to investment banking, and who was finally leaving her husband and children to be with me.

And I blew it. I rushed out of the house, ignoring my bodyguard, leapt into the car and turned the key in the ignition. I'm not quite sure what happened next, but I never got to see those perfectly white panties.

There were bad guys circling. Grossbank had seized the funds of a string of dodgy institutions who seemed to be a bit too close to the terrorist finance action. It wasn't that

I wanted to be a hero, just that they sort of pissed me off, and events took on a momentum of their own. I got on the wrong side of them and I suppose they wanted to make an example.

Two Livers reaches across to a bedside table and holds up a newspaper. It's the Post, and there's a photograph of two figures illuminated by a huge explosion in the background as a fireball engulfs a car. Shit. That was my car, my Bentley, with the personalised number plate, H1 PAY. 'Nine Lives Hart survives bomb, saves bodyguard'. I shake my head in bewilderment.

Two Livers touches my arm, reassuring, tender. 'It didn't go off properly.'

'What do you mean?'

'The police have told us. When you turned the key in the ignition, you set off the detonator. There must have been a small explosion, but it didn't set off the explosives under the fuel tank. At least not straight away. The bodyguard pulled you out and was dragging you away, when this happened.'

I look at the picture again. I vaguely recall being manhandled out of the car, leaning on someone strong, then another blast and we span around together – and were photographed. I take the newspaper and start reading despite the thumping in my head. We were photographed by a thirteen year old girl called Anna Mahaffey, who was walking along the street and just happened to have a camera on her mobile phone. She snapped what became the defining image of the Dave Hart car bombing, wired across the world to every newspaper and TV station. And she caught us spinning

6

around with the force of the explosion in that split second when it appeared the bodyguard was on top of me, and that I was carrying him.

Damn, I'm a hero. Again.

'You were pretty badly shaken up.'

'Sh – shaken up? What do you mean?' I point at the wires and the monitors. 'Y – you mean I wasn't injured?'

'No. Nothing more than a few scratches. You're in here now to deal with the drugs and the booze.'

\*　　　\*　　　\*

I'VE OFTEN heard it said – mostly by me – that compromise is the enemy of achievement. When it comes to PR, the best firm in the business is Ball Taittinger. They are quite simply the most shit hot outfit there is with the best connections and the most clout. If what you are doing requires the very best, then you hire these guys. For everything else, use an ordinary firm. They're reassuringly expensive, and I insist on paying top dollar. Or at least I insist on Grossbank paying top dollar. Naturally, I'm looked after by the super cool, sleek, grey-haired senior partner, a man in his early sixties with almost as many miles on the clock as I have myself – although I think my clock's been round the dial once already – and whom I call the Silver Fox.

Today the Silver Fox is going to help me deal with my drug habit, my alcoholism, and my addiction to sex.

I'm staying at the Abbey, a super-expensive, ultra-chic private hospital for the rich and famous, that specialises in addiction. The Abbey doesn't actually cure you of whatever it is you are addicted to – you have to do that yourself – but it's great PR, and with the right spin you can turn a problem into an opportunity. You're not weak, selfish, stupid and possibly criminal. You're a victim. People don't condemn you, they sympathise with you. And once you've done a few weeks out of the public eye, you can return once more to your normal abusive lifestyle.

The doctors here think I should be dead.

In a way that's kind of flattering. They keep bringing along young interns who stare at the readings and look at me with awe. On the other hand, I see it differently. The way I see it, I'm probably not the first investment banker to have suffered from the occasional moment of stress. Naturally, we all have different ways of dealing with it. Some unwind over a glass or two of whisky. Others get into drugs, with cocaine probably still the number one choice. Some prefer the comforts they can find in the arms of a beautiful woman – or two, or sometimes more. Being a very senior investment banker, and extremely rich and powerful – not to mention both stressed and greedy – I prefer all three, preferably at the same time.

The problem is that eventually it catches up with you.

And so instead of finally getting together with the love of my life, the gorgeous Sally Mills – who has left me a tearful voicemail saying our love 'is not to be' (we'll see about that) and that she has returned, distraught, to beg forgiveness from the under-achieving schoolteacher – I'm being prepped for an exclusive interview and a photo-shoot with Her Magazine.

I'm going to tell some dimwit airhead woman reporter that I wasn't shagging hookers every night for fun, but because I needed a release; that I got into drugs out of casual curiosity and I was snared before I knew it, and now I want to share my experience with young people everywhere. That part is true. I've a lot of experience I'd like to share with blonde seventeen year olds, but I'll be careful not to share that with the reporter. And finally I'll talk about the evils of drink. I have a particularly evil fifty-year-old Scotch in my bedside cabinet, but I'll keep it out of sight while we do the interview.

After that there'll be more interviews, eventually a TV appearance on Dick and Julie, and once it's all out in the open, I'll get back to work. I'm desperate to get back to work. I need to before the board realise quite how redundant I was before all this happened.

\*       \*       \*

FIVE TEDIOUS weeks have passed. Weeks that were boring beyond belief. The bastards took my whisky away. They wouldn't let me buy drugs. And sex was out of the question.

Can you believe that? And I was actually paying to be deprived.

I ended up working out maniacally in the gym, if only to escape the boredom, lost weight, shaped up, and found after a while that the cravings started to fade – or at least that's what I claimed with absolute sincerity in the group therapy sessions and the long conversations on a couch with my shrink. They say that addicts can be very cunning, but investment bankers are even smarter.

Yes, we're plausible.

And now it's over. The papers have all carried my story, the hero has sought and received redemption, and with the help of the Silver Fox, I'm going to make a triumphal return to Grossbank.

I've moved into an apartment in Whitehall Court, near the supposed safety of the heart of government, with well-patrolled streets and my own team of bodyguards. I still have Tom, my driver, well over six feet tall and built to impress, who drives me in an armoured S-class Mercedes. But we also have two other cars – Range Rovers – one of which drives ahead of us and one behind. In the Range Rovers are my bodyguards, whom I've called the Meat Factory. They are led by Scary Andy, a six-foot six-inch ex-Royal Marine weighing in at just over two hundred pounds. Arnie 'the Terminator' is not quite as tall, but even wider, and weighs in at two hundred and forty pounds. They are my regulars, but are supplemented by a whole team of human wardrobes.

Everywhere I go, I feel as if my little convoy creates its own hole in the ozone layer, three gas guzzlers complete with heavies to transport one greying, tired-looking, middle-aged man in a suit. How sad is that?

On the other hand, it works wonders for the ego, which is probably why politicians love it. On a good day it can feel totally Hollywood. Entering a room with a bunch of heavies wearing suits and dark glasses is rather like being in a scene from The Godfather. Better yet, it can feel positively Presidential. Sadly I won't ever be President of the United States, but there are times when I feel that being Dave Hart is the next best thing. The only bit I miss is the bag man, the uniformed officer with a briefcase containing the nuclear launch codes. Imagine if I had access to the nuclear launch codes. Then we'd really have a party…

And the aphrodisiac effect on women is remarkable. When I walk into a room surrounded by my wardrobes, all of whom are taller, stronger and manlier than me, guess who the ladies look at? That's right – the little guy in the middle, the one the heavies hold the door for.

But today is different. Today the heavies will stay in the background, as I stage-manage the final part of my rehabilitation: my triumphal return to the trading floor of the bank where I made my name.

We pull up outside the Grossbank building, and I pretend the press cameras and the TV crews aren't there as Tom helps me out of the car, passes me my crutches – yes, crutches – and I make my way painfully and bravely to the foyer, where Two Livers and my loyal team are waiting for me.

I look around the eager, smiling faces of my heads of department. Bastards.

I know they'll have been scheming. I'll leave it a couple of days to make them feel safe, then have a couple taken out and shot to encourage the others.

We go up in the lift to the sixth floor, where the sales and trading teams are and where I keep my corner office, looking out towards the Bank of England.

As I emerge onto the floor there's pandemonium, as all business stops and the traders cheer and whoop and high five each other. Isn't it wonderful? My people love me. The fact is, they couldn't have cared less about me, and why should they? Imagine the extra headroom in the bonus pool if I wasn't around to take the first slice.

I struggle manfully to my office, where Maria, my long-suffering, loyal secretary is waiting for me. Maria is mid-forties, heavily built, half German and a Grossbank lifer. She understands me – well, sort of – and we get on well. When I'm ten yards from her, I pause. A hush descends on the trading floor as I drop the crutches and walk slowly, painfully towards my office. In my head I'm playing the theme tune from *Chariots of Fire* as I drag myself one painful step at a time. Only when I get there do I catch hold of the doorframe and turn to wave to the troops. A great cheer goes up. I'm back, and the cameras have caught it all.

Once I'm inside my office Maria draws the blinds so I can wander over to the desk in privacy, put my feet up and light a cigar, blowing smoke rings at the 'No Smoking' sign on the wall.

\*       \*       \*

MY FIRST day back in the office passes slowly as I get up to speed with what's happened to the business while I was away.

Just as I feared, it's been going brilliantly, master-minded by my two key lieutenants, Two Livers, who handles all the corporate business, and Paul Ryan, the head of Markets, who looks after sales and trading. Paul is the Brad Pitt of Grossbank, tall, fit, good-looking, charming, but unlike Brad Pitt he's gay. I'm very pleased about Paul's sexual orientation. It means that out of the top three people running Grossbank in London, the only predatory heterosexual male is me.

Maria calls through on the intercom. I assume it's another 'welcome back' call from someone senior at another firm. I've been getting a lot of them. All the heads of the major firms have called, and I even had a bunch of roses from Tripod Turner, the biggest swinging dick of them all, Chief Investment Officer at the Boston International Group, the world's biggest investing institution. Herman Schwartz, the Frankfurt-based Chairman of Grossbank, has sent me a long, handwritten personal letter of welcome, and Two Livers has sent me an email saying she's so pleased to have me back that if I'm free tonight she'd like to invite me round to her place for a special treat. I like it when she gives me special treats.

'Who is it?'

'Mister Hart, I have Wendy on line three.'

Shit. Wendy is my ex-wife. She wants something. She'll have heard I'm back, and now she'll expect to resume normal milking activities – briefly paused while I was in recovery – and the pretext will be Samantha, our daughter, who has recently celebrated her fourth birthday. I couldn't actually make it in person, but I did send a van-load of presents, so this had better not be a complaint.

I flick the button on the speakerphone. 'Darling, how are you?'

'Wh – what? Dave, it's me – Wendy.'

'Wendy? Wendy who? But I thought – oh, shit…' I hang up and grin. That'll really piss her off.

Paul Ryan comes to see me. He's looking incredibly elegant in a way that no straight Englishman could ever manage – in fact a straight guy would have to be Italian to look this good – but he's come to say he's concerned about me.

'Dave – you can't carry on the way you were… you know… before all this happened.'

'What do you mean?'

'You know what I mean. The whole lifestyle thing. You were killing yourself. It simply isn't viable.' He's just a little wary, watching to see if he's overstepped the mark and I'm going to explode. He doesn't want to alienate the Golden Goose, but at the same time can't allow it to carry on mainlining heroin. 'I don't know if anyone else is going to tell you this, but I am. You have to change. You have to get this stuff under control.'

Damn, he's good. If I had a couple of scoring cards behind my desk I'd hold up ten points for sincerity. But then I check him out again and nobody's that good. He actually means it. Or have I lost my touch and I just can't read him anymore?

The problem for people who run investment banks is finding colleagues who are prepared to disagree with you – at least up to a point. This is why I like Paul and Two Livers so much. If you hand out tens of millions of pounds each year at bonus time, most people want to stay on the right side of you at all costs. Announce that you're planning to open an investment banking operation in Antarctica, and most of them will convince you you're a genius, a visionary who's ahead of the game and will steal a march on the competition.

'Paul, I know. I need to re-focus my priorities. Life isn't just about money. What's the point of having lots of money if all you do is count it?'

He's nodding, agreeing with me. I'm not sure quite where this is going, but I'm feeling relaxed, so I decide to press on.

'Sex is also important. And drugs. And of course

alcohol and fast cars, even if most of us don't know how to drive them properly.'

'No, Dave, no – don't go there. Dave, we're bankers. This isn't rock and roll.'

'Really?' I say this as if I kind of wish it was. Which maybe I do. He's got up and he's standing facing me. 'Dave, those things were destroying you.'

'Is that right?' I thought they stopped me getting bored. I was planning to treat this as a light-hearted piss-take and have a laugh. But he could be right. 'You may be right. Okay. Look – I'll ease up on the drink.'

'And the drugs.'

I nod. 'And the drugs.'

'And the hookers.'

'Okay, okay – I promise.' He strides round the desk and I get up quickly, wondering if he's going to attack me for taking the piss. But instead he embraces me, a big bone-crunching hug, and I smile broadly and squeeze him back.

'I give you my word, Paul. I'll ease up on the drink, the drugs and the hookers.'

At least before lunch.

\*　　　\*　　　\*

I'M BORED. This was always my problem in the past, and it's even worse now. The thing about being in charge is that you don't really have to do anything. Sure, you can fill your days with meetings, where your subordinates brief you on things and try to look good (but for what – so you can pay them more?), or you meet clients and shake their hands and mouth platitudes to convince them that their business is important to the bonus pool – I mean, the firm – or hold morale boosting 'town hall' meetings where you patronise junior employees by reading out 'key corporate messages' prepared by the Human Resources Department or the worker bees in Corporate Communications – 'one dream, one team, one firm' – or some such twaddle. It would all seem so futile, if it weren't for the millions of pounds I get paid for doing it.

In an attempt to raise my spirits, Paul and Two Livers are taking me to the Berkmann Schliebowitz drinks party. It's a modest bash hosted by one of Wall Street's most successful firms for their five hundred closest friends in the London market. It's being held at the Embalmers' Hall, one of the oldest livery companies in the City of London, and anyone who is anyone in the Square Mile will be there. Champagne, ice sculptures, entertainers – I can hardly wait.

Tom drops us off about half an hour after the due time, mainly because they had to twist my arm to go. I'm in a foul mood. I haven't had sex all day, my nose is running and my mouth is dry. I could fix all this in a couple of phone calls, but they won't let me.

So instead we find ourselves waiting in line to collect our name badges from a pretty girl at the reception desk, behind a very tall, mid-thirties, balding American with a deep booming voice and a very athletic figure. He's the sort of man who exudes certainty – you just know he was a college football star, got all the top grades, comes from a privileged family, probably 'East Coast aristocracy', and he has what the Americans call Big Verbal Presence: take him to a meeting, any meeting, even if he knows nothing at all about what's being discussed, and he'll talk a lot at great volume and Be Impressive. These days, this is what the American investment banks like – quiet, short, thoughtful people need not apply.

Right now, he's being Verbally Massive with the receptionist, who is trying to be polite but is obviously flustered.

'The name is Hurst. H – U – R – S – T. That's G. Herbert Hurst the Third. From Schleppenheim. That's Schleppenheim with an S. I'm head of Derivatives. That's with a D.'

He says all this in a slowed down, 'I'm talking to a moron' manner. The receptionist blushes delightfully and looks flustered. I guess she's about twenty-three, quite pretty with a trim figure and a cute butt, and from the sound of her accent, comes from Poland. She's probably getting the minimum wage, working nights to earn money and putting up with shit from the likes of G. Herbert. She looks at him helplessly. There isn't a name badge for him, although he is on the list.

'I'm very sorry. This won't take a moment.'

Exasperated, he turns to us as the next in line, does a double-take when he sees Two Livers and raises his eyes heavenwards, as if trying to elicit some sympathy at the nonsense that People Like Us sometimes have to suffer at the hands of the merely mortal. Two Livers stares right through him.

The receptionist goes to make him up a badge, but he ignores her and walks past.

'I think most of the people here know who I am.'

Wanker. I look at Two Livers and Paul and we nod to

each other. If they didn't know who G. Herbert Hurst the Third was before tonight, they certainly will in about thirty minutes. As we take our badges, I growl to the others, 'Let's nail the motherfucker.'

We peel off in different directions, Paul seeking out the trading types while Two Livers and I head for the bar. She's wearing a skirt and jacket by Chanel, flatteringly snug in all the right places, without being in any way revealing, shoes by Jimmy Choo and jewellery by Kiki McDonough. Heads turn as we pass, and they aren't looking at me.

We get to the bar, where I catch the barman's eye and nod towards Two Livers: 'Fill her up.' At first he doesn't understand, then Two Livers leans forward and whispers something in his ear, and he scurries off, returning with two mojitos, and hands them both to her. She heads off into the crowd, doing the old 'excuse me, I'm taking this drink to a friend', so she can briefly mumble to the tedious, while staying on the move to nail down our prey.

I take a glass of champagne and wander over to the corner of the room, where some of the senior people are holding court.

Dan Harriman is talking to Clive Gunn, who runs the sales trading side of Prince's, and a tall, early forties, fair-haired guy I don't recognise.

'Hey Dave – come on over. Let me introduce you.'

Dan is heavily overweight, sweating, and looks like he's had about four martinis too many. 'Dave Hart, from Grossbank, this is Vladimir Kommisarov, from First Siberian Bank.'

Vlad the Impaler is well-known in the markets, though

I've never met him before. He gets his nickname not because he's an aggressive trader, but from his alleged prowess with the ladies. He's been sent by his masters in the Kremlin to set up a heavyweight investment banking operation in London. He has a firm grip and nods respectfully. 'I've heard a lot about you, Mister Hart. You are truly an amazing man.'

Wow – how about that for an opening line? I like him already. And I like his bank. The Russians have hit London in force, and are setting up investment banking operations to take on all-comers. Amongst the Russians, OneSib, as they are known in the market, are the biggest. Vlad has deep pockets behind him and a serious game to play. They are planning to hire two hundred professionals for their London operation and he's definitely in the market for talent. In no time at all we are getting on like a house on fire, talking the talk the way heads of investment banks do, swapping tales of business trips to the Ukraine – 'Six in a bed – at the same time? Really? It must have been a huge bed' – and sharing addresses and phone numbers in London – 'Are they really twins? And they make you watch first? Hot candle wax where?'

And then across the room I spot G. Herbert, clutching an orange juice and sharing his wisdom with a couple of shorter guys from other firms. I point him out to the others.

'Do you know him?'

Dan and Vlad don't know him, but Clive does. 'We deal with him a bit on the derivatives side. Seems sharp enough.'

I tap the side of my nose. 'Not as sharp as he should be.

Word has it – and this could be complete bullshit – that Schleppenheim could make a third quarter loss on the back of some of his trades.'

'Really?'

I nod knowingly. 'They're putting a brave face on it, running fast to make good their bad positions. It's not impossible they'll dig their way out and no one will ever know. But let's just say he may not have a long term future round there.' I snort. 'Or anywhere.'

Vlad seems stunned. 'But he is said to be very bright.' Vlad obviously does know him after all, or at least the headhunter who's been retained to hire OneSib's two hundred new employees does.

I wink and pat him on the back. 'All I'll say is let the buyer beware.' I tap the side of my nose again. 'Trust me on this one.'

Behind me, Two Livers is standing by the bar, doing tequila slammers with a couple of corporate finance types from one of the US firms. The guys are already unsteady on their feet, perspiring and starting to slur their words. They have no idea who they are drinking with. As I pass, I see them looking at G. Herbert as she speaks.

'...and I've heard there are three lawsuits in the process of being settled already. Quietly, obviously. No firm wants publicity like that. He just can't keep it zipped up.'

They seem amazed. 'But he always comes across as such a straight type. We go to the same gym. He works out pretty hard, plays golf at the weekend. Single, no girlfriend as far as I know. Pretty boring if you ask me. He's certainly serious about his career.'

'No girlfriend? Maybe that's why he keeps misbehaving

at work. But these days you just can't do that stuff. Not unless you're really senior.'

I head to the bar for a refill, and pass Paul Ryan talking to an obviously gay – which is to say incredibly good-looking and immaculately turned out – Asian guy who I remember as head of Debt Capital Markets at Samara Bank. They are also looking at G. Herbert.

'...sure I've seen him cruising. He often comes to the Sugar Club late on a Friday night. He does this big thing at work about being straight, but once he's done a few lines, well...'

'So he's a user?' The Asian guy looks disdainful. He obviously doesn't approve.

'Big time.' Paul sniffs theatrically. 'Loves the stuff.'

And so it goes on. We work the crowd, pleased to have something worthwhile to do on what might otherwise have been a routine occasion. When we eventually leave, ten minutes after our deadline, G. Herbert is standing alone in the centre of the room. He's somehow morphed into the social equivalent of the Invisible Man, finding it strangely hard to get anyone to catch his eye, despite seeing so many familiar faces in the crowd. He's dimly aware that all around him huddled conversations are taking place and strange looks are coming his way. There's a peculiar vibe tonight, and he can't quite put his finger on it. In fact if he didn't know better he'd be paranoid. Christ, I love my job.

\*     \*     \*

TWO LIVERS is angry. I only made it into the office at three in the afternoon, after an all night party. I don't feel exactly brilliant, though I have a feeling that if only I could remember where I went and what I was doing, I must have had a great time. I sit at my desk, trying to look as if I'm concentrating, while all the time resisting the urge to run to the bathroom and throw up.

'Earth to Dave…hello? Is anyone there? Dave, be honest. You're never going to change, are you?'

I shrug and try to look pitiful, which is not too hard with a brass band marching up and down in my head. 'I might get worse.'

I'm not sure if I meant it as a joke, but if I did, it didn't work.

'Dave, you're bored. You know it and I know it. You need a challenge, something to get you interested again, something to engage you.'

She's right. I am incredibly bored. The investment banking business is doing fantastically well, Herman and the board keep sending me messages of congratulation and invitations to ever more boring celebratory dinners in Frankfurt, but I really have no interest. I keep thinking about Sally, the love of my life, who has changed her phone number, returns my letters unopened, and refuses all contact. Bloody women. You can't live with them, but I certainly can't live without this one – at least not until I finally get inside those perfectly white panties.

It's strange how the mind works. Sometimes the subconscious makes connections in a way that the rational intellect would find impossible. Perfectly white panties make me think of the lingerie worn by the women I've slept with recently, all of which was dark coloured or black. I struggle to think of a non-G-string-wearing woman with traditional white cotton panties, and the last one I recall sleeping with was… French. And one thought leads to another.

'I've got an idea.'

'What sort of idea?' She has an expectant twinkle in her eye, and I don't think it's to do with sex. Sometimes I really can surprise her.

'I've been thinking about it for a while.' About five seconds, actually. 'We're going to do what Grossbank should have done long ago. A major strategic move. What the Germans do best.'

'What's that?'

'We're going to invade France.'

Two Livers' eyes widen and she takes a sharp intake of breath. I love it when she does that.

I flick the switch on the intercom. 'Maria – get me the Silver Fox!'

\*　　　\*　　　\*

INVESTMENT BANKING is ninety per cent form and ten per cent substance. My rivals say I've always hired the best to deal with the form, taking care of the substances myself, but that's just sour grapes. However, it is true that the most important events in life require the most meticulous stage management.

And nothing beats a good invasion.

We're not actually going to invade the whole of France, just one of the bastions of its financial community, Société Financière de Paris, or SFP for short. SFP is a stock broking and investment banking business headquartered in a fantastic old building not far from the Louvre. It employs a couple of thousand people, and – very importantly for me – its shares are listed on the Paris Bourse. First thing Monday morning its share price goes haywire. Someone is in there buying SFP stock like it's going out of fashion. It is what used to be called a dawn raid – we go in hard and early, taking everyone by surprise, acquire as big a position as we can manage, then announce we are there and see what happens.

When we disclose that Grossbank has a fifteen per cent stake in SFP, the price goes even higher. The financial press are all over us, demanding to know if taking this stake is a prelude to something bigger, and we actually intend to make a takeover bid for one of France's oldest established financial institutions, a firm whose name is synonymous with the French establishment.

Naturally, guided by the Silver Fox, we say nothing. 'Any comment at this time would be inappropriate. However, we look forward to fruitful discussions with the board of SFP in the coming days on matters of mutual interest.' That sends the stock up another five per cent.

On the Wednesday morning I fly in to Paris with Two Livers and Paul Ryan. Grossbank has its own Paris-based operation, and the team there meet us and we head off in a convoy of black limousines for the SFP headquarters.

When we get there, even I'm impressed. The entrance hall is enormous, with marble floors, huge columns going up to a vaulted ceiling, and magnificent oils on the walls. It feels more like the Presidential palace than an investment bank. If the intention is to impress clients arriving here, it certainly works.

We are shown up to the fifth floor, to another enormous anteroom full of antique furniture, where the loudest noise is the ticking of ancient clocks. A pretty assistant sits at a desk in absolute silence, until a full fifteen minutes have passed, and then gets up – apparently without being signalled to do so – and invites us to follow her into the boardroom.

She opens massive double doors and we go into a large conference room with an oval table, around which fifteen elderly men are seated. The Chairman, Jean-Marie LeGrand, a portly, bald septuagenarian, remains seated, staring at us as if it's 1940 all over again and we've arrived to take their surrender. I look around the room. None of the others will meet my glance. No one gets up to shake our hands or introduce themselves. There are three empty chairs at the far end of the table, and the assistant directs us to take a seat.

LeGrand clears his throat and speaks very slowly. 'So, Monsieur 'art... welcome to Paris.'

Oh, the French do so love their irony. It's about as chilly a welcome as he could give without actually throwing us out. I feel I should do something to break the ice, like telling a joke. 'Gentlemen, do you know how many Frenchmen it takes to defend Paris? No? Neither do I. In fact no one does. Because they've never tried.' On reflection, it wouldn't be a great start. And I do want this to start well, even though it may end differently.

'Thank you, Monsieur LeGrand. My colleagues and I are delighted to be here. Please let me introduce, on my left, Laura MacKay, head of Corporates at Grossbank...' Being Frenchmen, they cannot help but scrutinise Two Livers and nod their approval. '...and on my right, Paul Ryan, head of Markets.'

Paul gets a cursory glance from a couple of them, but mostly they stay looking at Two Livers. I pause and look around the room, doing my 'cheerfully optimistic, possibly just a little bit naive, but fundamentally has his heart in the right place' impression. 'Thank you for agreeing to see us today. May I say a few words?'

LeGrand nods and waves his hand casually, obviously comfortable sitting at the head of his own board table. 'Of course, Monsieur – if you believe you 'ave something of interest or relevance to propose to us.' He says this with utter contempt. How could we possibly have anything interesting to say? We're foreigners, after all.

I look down at the table, pause to collect my thoughts and compose myself, because I need to keep a straight face. I look up.

'Gentlemen, France is a great nation.'

You can hear a pin drop. All of them are staring at me. I have their full attention. I say the next part very slowly.

'The reason that France is a great nation, is because the French are a great people.'

Now I've got them. They love me. Whatever I say next really does not matter. I could spend half an hour reading from the telephone directory and all they would remember would be the two opening lines. Gotcha.

I go on to say that because France is such a major nation, a centre of influence and power, a place of cultural sophistication punching well above its considerable weight, Grossbank needs not just a presence in the Paris market, but a leading position. We could grow our own business, but it would take years. Or we could buy into an existing firm and draw up a co-operation agreement that would work to our mutual benefit. We have chosen the latter course, and since we are only interested in the very best, we have come to SFP.

The way to a Frenchman's heart is via his ego. Sometimes their egos are enormous, so pander to them. In the case of a very senior Establishment Frenchman like LeGrand, getting him and his ego in the room at the same time can be quite a challenge. But I think I've managed it.

LeGrand finally gets up, comes down to the far end of the table, and with a broad smile shakes my hand and embraces me. I can even smell his after-shave, which I disapprove of. I'm wearing Eau de Jade from the Armani Black Collection, and I hope he appreciates it. He then gives Paul a brief handshake, and Two Livers gets an even bigger embrace than I did. The other board members take their cue and get up to shake hands with Paul and me and line up to take turns embracing Two Livers, who makes sure she doesn't make eye contact with me, in case we both crack up.

\*     \*     \*

I WAS only partly bullshitting in what I said about France. I do in fact love the place. I love the mountains, the beaches, the vineyards, the wide open spaces. On an individual basis, I even like some of the people. Well, some of the women anyway. The problem is that collectively they are a pain in the arse, a bunch of absurdly strutting cockerels, who cling to past glories in a way that makes the Brits seem forward-looking, and assert their independence by being as difficult as they can about any issue you care to name.

Do you remember the neutron bomb? It was a Cold War invention, a 'clean' nuclear device that did not cause much physical blast damage, but could penetrate buildings and tank armour and irradiate the people inside. It was a nuclear weapon that might actually have been used, if the Soviet armies had ever rolled forward into West Germany, because the radiation decayed in a few days, leaving the countryside pristine, but rather quiet. The codename was 'Instant Sunshine'. I have a theory about the neutron bomb. I don't think it was meant for the Russians at all. France is the nation for which God gave us the neutron bomb.

Having sweet-talked the board, we now sit down at 'working level' and spend a couple of days thrashing out a co-operation agreement. We agree to raise Grossbank's stake in SFP to twenty-five per cent, but on a friendly, pre-announced basis. At the same time we will merge Grossbank's fledgling French business into SFP. I will join the SFP board, and the two firms will invest together in expanding the share trading business, under the new co-heads of French equities, Werner Grubmann from Grossbank, and Olivier Martin from SFP.

Mutual expressions of goodwill are exchanged between our two great firms, there is respect and trust on both sides, and we look forward to a bright future together based on a clear alignment of interests. Truly everything is for the best in the best of all possible worlds.

Yeah, right.

Werner Grubmann is hand-picked by me. He knows nothing about the Paris Bourse, but he could run a mean concentration camp. He has the look of a Hollywood villain straight from central casting. Shaven-headed, tall and muscular; even by German standards he has a limited sense of humour. He also has toxic halitosis, which is so bad he could be Germany's secret weapon. Send him into the caves at Tora Bora and he'd clean out the Taliban in twenty minutes. And like everyone I've ever met who is afflicted in this way, he has no sense of personal space, but loves to crowd up close to you.

Olivier Martin on the other hand, is short, skinny, fastidious, intellectual and fancies that he has a superb sense of ironic humour. Clearly, they are a match made in heaven.

*     *     *

BACK IN the office in London, I feel as if I've lit the blue touch paper. Now all I have to do is stand back and wait for the explosion. But just in case, I hire in a specialist media consultant, Ed Black of Black Associates, to work quietly alongside the Silver Fox, doing the things that he wouldn't.

That may have something to do with the French press somehow getting hold of the story that the SFP building has been earmarked by Grossbank's real estate division for re-development. Somehow architectural drawings found their way into the hands of the media showing how much more valuable this prime site would be as a multi-storey car park.

Naturally the Mayor of Paris denies that this proposal even exists, and insists that if it did, he would never grant permission for the destruction and redevelopment of a historic landmark building. But then he would say that, wouldn't he? And a couple of days later the real story breaks. SFP is to be cleared out to make way for a new American Embassy.

This one plays really well in the French press. The French just love the Americans. When the Mayor of Paris and the US Ambassador jointly deny that there is any such plan, everyone knows it must be true.

And then there's the internet. On the internet, some wag has posted shots of what is claimed to be Grossbank's fleet of corporate jets lined up at Orly Airport. We call them smokers, and we really do have a lot of them – I sometimes joke that I don't have a jet, I have an entire air force.

The shots on the internet show a row of sleek, white Gulfstream jets with black crosses on their fuselages. As if Grossbank would actually paint black crosses on the sides of its planes – only a semi-hysterical, paranoid Frenchman could believe such a thing. But some of them do seem to be both paranoid and hysterical, and they are circulating by email shots of what they call the 'Grossbank Luftwaffe'.

Meanwhile round at SFP the anti-German feeling is being fuelled by Werner Grubmann and the Grossbank team who are working with him on Projekt Adler – Project Eagle, as we have chosen to call it for friendly historical reasons.

On day three I get the first call from LeGrand. He's hesitant about raising a delicate matter of personal style, but a number of his senior people have come to him to ask if he has noticed how Werner and the Grossbank team – who are all hand-picked from Frankfurt, and all of a similar build and stature to Werner – walk in step when they move around the building, and never knock before opening doors.

I play the innocent. 'Jean-Marie, why are you people concerned? At Grossbank we don't believe in knocking on people's office doors. We believe in an open culture of trust and transparency. I told Werner myself, I said don't be hesitant, just throw their doors open and smile, and say 'We're from Grossbank and we're here to help you'. That's our style. I always say my door is open for everyone. No one has anything to hide. Do your people have something to hide?'

'Of course not,' he blusters, 'but it is like the old films of the Gestapo in the war. The door bursts open and they all come in. Sometimes six or eight of them at a time. My 'eads of department are not used to this.'

I assure him that these are minor teething problems, and the cultural fit will work itself out in no time. Germany and France have always been close, and are really a great natural match, aren't they? I suggest he focuses more on fixing the press. Who is it, who is stirring up all this anti-German feeling?

His next call is more serious.

'Dave, your people 'ere are too aggressive. This cannot continue. My best people will leave. 'alf of them already believe the firm is to be closed to make way for the new American Embassy, and now this – it is too much.'

'Talk to me, Jean-Marie. Tell me what happened.'

He pauses, apparently flustered, collecting his thoughts. 'It is Grubmann.'

'You mean Werner? Isn't he great? He's a really good

guy. I love him. And we've got lots like him. Thousands, in fact, and you'd be amazed how many are asking to be posted to Paris. This is so exciting.'

There's a long pause at the other end, and I have the feeling that LeGrand is imagining thousands of shaven headed Germans marching in step down the Champs-Elysées, square-jawed and grim-faced, repeating over and over in strong, guttural accents: 'Ve are from Grossbank and ve are here to help you.'

'Dave – Werner has proposed that we sell the corporate art collection.'

There's a long silence. He probably thinks I have to pick myself up from the floor after such a bombshell.

'Not only that. He thinks we must sell the wine cellar too.'

Wow. Werner doesn't mess around. Go in hard, and go for the jugular. Never forget, these guys invaded Russia.

'Great, I think those are both really good ideas. I've heard you've got some real treasures on the walls there. And more in the cellars. Worth millions. We could make a real killing. Think of the bonus pool, Jean-Marie.'

I think I hear a gasp down the telephone, followed by an even longer silence.

'Jean-Marie – are you there?'

'Click. Brrrrr…'

Gotcha.

Now it's only a matter of time.

\* \* \*

THE PROBLEM with real life, is that things all happen at once. Just as I'm reaching the end game with my invasion of

France, I'm brought down to earth with a bump. I've just hired a very expensive Head of Diversity for the Human Resources department in London, called Melissa Myers.

Melissa is a gorgeous mid-thirties brunette with a legal background and a fabulous figure with a sexy, hip-swinging walk that blows me away. She was previously at Prince's, but as soon as I saw her I knew that I had to have her, so I doubled her money and gave her a three-year guarantee. Her role at Grossbank will be to ensure that all minorities in the workplace, but in particular women employees, are treated with appropriate dignity and respect at all levels of the organisation.

Today is her first day and I'm bending her over my desk – the blinds are closed and the little red 'Do not disturb' light is on over the door – and I'm trying her out from behind. Just as I'm about to explode, the door bursts open and Two Livers storms in. She's furious.

'Dave – get that thing off your penis and take a look at this.'

Beneath me, Melissa gasps, tenses, and I have a sudden fear of her going into spasm, clamping me tightly inside her and locking us together. I have client meetings today and even I couldn't do them like this.

Most men would panic. I smile. 'Have you two met? Melissa, this is Laura MacKay, Head of Corporates. Two Livers, this is Melissa…'

Two Livers ignores her. 'Dave, cut the crap and look at this.'

She tosses a piece of paper on the desk next to the brunette, who is disengaging, mercifully allowing me to slide free, and pulls her skirt down, tries to straighten her hair and struggles to find something to say, but then realises that Two Livers and I are both ignoring her and takes flight from my office without saying a word. I turn away from Two Livers, remove my condom and zip myself up, then toss it in the bin under the desk. There are two others there already – it's been a busy morning.

The paper is a Court Order, from the local sheriff's court in Banffshire, where Sally Mills is living.

'Compliance and Legal formally took receipt of it, but when they saw what it was they brought it to me. Dave, Sally Mills and her husband are saying you've been harassing her. And now the court are ordering you to have no further contact, direct or indirect. She's a married woman and wants to stay that way.'

Damn. I flop down into my chair and pick up the Court Order again to read it through. 'Harassment – what do they mean, harassment? I haven't been harassing her.'

Two Livers takes a seat opposite me. 'So what have you been doing?'

I shrug nonchalantly, but knowing that I won't get away with lying. 'I've been sending flowers.'

'How often?'

I shrug again. 'From time to time.'

'How often?'

I get up and start to pace around the office. I hate it when she interrogates me. 'Every day.'

'Every day?'

'That's right. Every day. I wanted to keep the memory of me fresh in her mind.'

'No wonder she feels harassed. Have you been doing anything else?'

'Gifts.'

'Gifts? What kind of gifts?'

I wave my hands helplessly. 'You know the sort of thing – Tiffany, Bulgari, Chanel... the kind of things I imagined a woman wouldn't necessarily find in Banffshire.'

'What were they worth, these gifts?'

'Don't ask me – I didn't count. I expensed them.'

'But you must know roughly.'

'Roughly? Oh, roughly... hundreds...'

'Hundreds?'

'...of thousands... More than a teacher makes, anyway.'

'Jesus, Dave – you sent her flowers every day, and hundreds of thousands of pounds of gifts?'

'All of which she returned.'

'She returned them? What kind of whacko is she? Was there anything else?'

'Not really. Well, except for the plane.'

'The plane?'

'I hired a plane.'

'What for?'

'To circle round her house with a sky sign.'

'A sky sign? Dave, are you mad?'

I nod. 'Madly in love, yes.'

'What did the sign say?'

'Oh, nothing very original. Sally I love you, Sally our love will never die, stuff like that. I heard it got into the local papers.'

'You really are insane. No wonder she's feeling harassed.'

'What can I do?'

'Draw a line, Dave. The past is the past. The moment's gone.' She gets up and stands close to me. I can smell her scent, and feel a stirring from the unfinished business she interrupted. I glance at my watch. My next meeting is in twenty minutes, but I don't care if I'm late. 'Oh, all right…'

*       *       *

I LOVE the Square Mile. It's seven a.m. and I'm walking down Threadneedle Street, bodyguards on either side of me to part the crowds of pin stripes hurrying to their workstations. Take a deep breath and what can you smell? Money. It's hanging in the air so thickly you can almost taste it. At times like this the City of London has to be the best place on earth.

I spent last night with Anya from Helsinki, a twenty-two year old student hoping one day to become an architect – yeah, right – and Anne from Sussex, an actress who's between jobs – yeah, yeah. What they had in common, apart from working for the same escort agency and being great in bed, is a passably similar name. I'm finding it harder to remember their names these days, so my new approach is to call up girls with names that sound similar, or at least start with the same letter.

Do you think I'm wrong to pay for sex? Don't kid yourself. We all pay for sex. One way or another. It's just that I do it on my own terms, and I try to stay in control.

I'm running fifteen minutes later than planned. Tom got stuck in traffic, so I got out and walked. According to the radio some American banker called Hurst tried to end it all by jumping off Blackfriars Bridge. Loser couldn't even get that right, and the river police had to fish him out, causing hold-ups all the way along the Embankment. His name rings a bell, but I can't quite place it. They said on the radio he'd sent an email to his boss, who had recently given him notice to quit, claiming his life was in ruins, he'd lost all his friends, everyone had it in for him, and he just couldn't take it anymore. Damned inconsiderate to hold up the early morning traffic.

I'm about to enter the bank, when my mobile phone goes off. It's Jean-Marie LeGrand. He's finally had it with the Germans. It didn't take as long as I thought. The French never did have much stomach for a fight. I call Maria to change my plans and get a private jet organised to take me to Paris. It's show time.

\*  \*  \*

I'M MARCHING down the corridor towards LeGrand's office. Werner and his team are flanking me, and yes, they do all march in step. Is this a natural German instinct? It's kind of scary, and makes me walk faster, which in turn makes them speed up, until we are all hurtling down the corridor, throw open the doors, storm past the secretaries in the outer office and burst in on LeGrand, who leaps up from his desk, speechless with fear and surprise. I smile.

'Jean-Marie – how good to see you.' I hold out my hand, but he makes no move to shake it.

'Dave – please ask your colleagues to leave my office immediately.'

I turn to Werner and the team and nod to them to leave. Werner doesn't quite click his heels, but we can all tell that that's what he wants to do. He does what I suppose he imagines is an impression of someone smiling and nods towards LeGrand, who steps back from the desk to avoid a wave of deadly, toxic halitosis. It was Jean-Paul Sartre who wrote that hell is other people. In Paris, it's more specific than that. Hell is Werner Grubmann – Christ, he's done a great job.

When the team have left, I sit down. 'What is it, Jean-Marie?'

He looks beaten. 'Dave, this strategic co-operation between SFP and Grossbank has been a catastrophe.'

'Really? I thought it was going rather well. We have people queuing up to come over here.'

He shakes his head and stares at the blotter on his desk. 'You 'ave to understand, Dave. We are a proud people with a great past.' Yeah, right. I do the jokes around here. 'Dave, it 'as not worked at all. And we cannot continue. I 'ave 'ad representations from the Finance Ministry, and from the regulatory authorities.'

'What sort of representations, Jean-Marie?'

'There are certain people… people who are very senior in the administration… people who prefer not to see SFP fall under the influence of a foreign bank.'

'Really? Why on earth is that?'

He gives me a short, sharp look, checking to see if I'm taking the piss. 'These people 'ave great influence. And they 'ave decided that there should be a merger between SFP and the Banque du Nord. It will be announced shortly. Both boards will sign today. Grossbank's shares in

SFP will be acquired by Banque du Nord for a substantial premium, but our co-operation must end.'

I sit back, amazed. 'No – are you saying that someone high up in the government, in the French Establishment, has leant on Banque du Nord to buy out SFP just to keep the Germans away? And they're paying for the privilege? You must be kidding. I thought the French wanted nothing more than to be in bed with the Germans.'

He squirms and I try not to grin. It's the French way. Yes, they are open to foreigners coming into their markets, but only on their terms. Sure, they'd love to be in bed with the Germans, but guess who'd be biting the pillow and who'd be wearing the condom. It's their patch and they call the shots, and who can blame them for that? Certainly not Grossbank's shareholders. A quick back of the envelope calculation in the car on the way to the airport shows us looking at half a billion euros profit. I might even give Werner a bonus.

*       *       *

I'M BACK in London. The fact is that while it was fun to have a go at the French, and we made an enormous profit, I'm genuinely minded to take over another firm.

This is not to say that when banks buy one another, it's necessarily good news for shareholders or the firms themselves. In fact when investment banks buy one another, it's usually the most wasteful, shareholder value-destroying exercise seen in the corporate world.

The investment bankers themselves do well out of it, getting fat payouts, lock-ins, guarantees and early vestings of share-incentive schemes – getting rich, in other words –

but within a couple of years it usually becomes apparent that there were no synergies, that the best people have left anyway, and the acquirer wasted its money. Fortunately by then the people who took the decisions will have moved on to other firms or retired to their yachts and their places in the sun.

In my particular case, I have a different reason to contemplate taking over another firm. The firm I have in mind is Bartons. We all have our demons to slay, and many of mine come from the years I spent working for Rory, my fair-haired, blue-eyed boy wonder of a boss at Bartons, and Sir Oliver Barton, the Chairman and controlling family shareholder. Without the fear and insecurity ingrained into me at Bartons, I could be a well-balanced human being. Well, almost.

So today I'm meeting Sir Oliver for lunch at the City of London Club. Sir Oliver doesn't actually give a shit about me. He probably doesn't even remember me from when I was at Bartons, though he has certainly heard about me since. He greets me in the bar of the Club like a long-lost friend, all smiles and bonhomie and two-handed handshakes.

The reason Sir Oliver is meeting me has nothing to do with Dave Hart, and everything to do with the Grossbank Panzer Division parked outside, engines idling, crews wondering where we're going next. Are we off to invade Poland, or France, or Bartons?

I love my Panzer Division. In an ideal world, everyone would have one. Luckily we don't have an ideal world. In the real world, I have a Panzer Division and Sir Oliver doesn't.

The deal is done remarkably easily. A hundred and fifty years of British banking history are carved up before dessert. Sir Oliver wants out. So do the rest of the family. In the investment banking world, Bartons is neither fish nor fowl: too big to be a niche player, nimbly moving from one opportunity to another, and too small to compete with the big boys, like the Americans whose operations are underpinned by their hugely profitable domestic businesses, or the Europeans with their massive balance sheets.

And there's another reason: Bartons own the freehold of their building near Liverpool Street Station. It's a ten storey building built in the early eighties, and is exactly the kind of prime real estate that the Corporation of London would love to see re-developed into, say, a modern, landscape defining, thirty storey tower.

Forget struggling, low quality earnings from corporate finance and stock broking, with high overhead employees demanding ever greater bonuses. Think instead demolition and re-development. No Parisian scare stories here. This is the real deal. When Sir Oliver and I shake hands over coffee, I agree that he and the family keep a share of the profits from the re-development of the site. He agrees that I get to press the plunger.

The way these deals work is that the Big Guys – in this case Sir Oliver and myself – agree the headline terms, and then 'our people' – the little people, the lawyers and the accountants – get to make it happen. Making it happen in this case will take several months, but I'm nothing if not impatient, and I have one task that can't wait several days, let alone several months. After lunch, I return with Sir Oliver to his office and he summons Rory.

It takes Rory all of five minutes to come bounding up to the tenth floor, tail wagging with puppy-like eagerness to please. I stand facing out over the City, as the door opens and Rory enters.

'Sir Oliver – I understand you wanted to see me.'

Sir Oliver is seated at his enormous power desk, staring idly at some screens off to one side. He nods distractedly. 'There's someone I wanted you to meet. Your prospective new boss.'

On cue, I turn to Rory and smile. It's a moment to treasure. He's frozen, standing in the centre of the room, immaculate in his Savile Row suit and Hermes tie. As he sees me, the smile fades from his face.

'D – Dave...'

'Rory.' My smile broadens, and I advance towards him, hand outstretched. We shake hands in the middle of Sir Oliver's office, and I'm delighted to note that his handshake is weak and clammy. I lean forward so my face is close to his. 'It's been a while. How are you?'

He swallows and looks to Sir Oliver for some explanation. 'I'm well, thank you. Sir Oliver, did you say my new boss?' His voice seems to have risen a couple of octaves.

Sir Oliver is still looking at numbers on one of the screens by his desk, or at least pretending to. 'Yes. But owner might be a better term. Grossbank are buying Bartons. Dave will be in charge.'

Rory stares at me, a mixture of disbelief, fear and hatred playing across his features. I smile. The vampire has returned.

\*     \*     \*

THE SILVER Fox is chatting amiably to some City reporters in the large conference room at Bartons. I spent many unhappy hours here, squirming nervously while Rory or Sir Oliver or other members of senior management lectured us on the latest round of imminent job cuts, the new expenses policy for members of the firm not senior enough to sit on the Management Committee, or the decision to merge different parts of the business to achieve greater synergy, for which read cost – i.e. people – savings.

Today is different. Today the Bartons conference room is covered in the Grossbank livery. Our logos are everywhere, and Bartons' have been airbrushed out.

The room is filling up nicely, as the big business story of the day is about to unfold. The last independent British investment bank is being bought by the Germans. Eight weeks have passed since Sir Oliver and I had lunch and the little people from Team Xerox have been working hard. This morning the official announcements went out, a collective gasp of horror came from the trading floor at Bartons, while high fives were exchanged on the floor at Grossbank, followed by an influx of phone calls to their opposite numbers at Bartons from our traders, explaining how many sugars they take in their coffee, and would they please say after me, 'Grossbank rocks'.

I enjoy the theatrical aspects of occasions like this. When the room is full I wait a further five minutes, then Sir Oliver and I sweep into the conference room from the rear, flanked by Two Livers and Paul Ryan, and followed by Rory, who is carrying a pile of hard copies of the PowerPoint presentation we are about to deliver, and which somehow got left behind by the presentation team. In my mind, I can hear someone announcing 'Ladies and gentlemen, the President of the United States', and indeed, such is the power of theatre that the press do actually stand up as we come in.

We go up onto the podium, and Sir Oliver and I sit in centre stage, with Two Livers and Paul on either side of us. Rory steps up onto the stage last, carrying the presentations, only to find that there is not a chair for him, which we ignore while he finds a free space on the podium to leave the presentations, then awkwardly steps down and stands beside the stage, pretending not to hear the tittering from the hacks.

'Ladies and gentlemen, welcome to Grossbank.' It's crass, but I can't resist it. 'This morning Sir Oliver Barton and I jointly announced a major event in the development of London as the leading financial centre in the world. Grossbank, itself one of the world's largest financial institutions, is merging its investment banking business with Bartons, taking over Bartons in its entirety, and at the same time planning significant moves to accelerate the growth and development of the two firms' joint business.' I pause and look out at a sea of scribbling hacks. I glance at Rory, who looks away nervously as I continue. 'It will come as no surprise to you that the combined investment banking business of Grossbank and Bartons, the Grossbank-Bartons business, will be known in future as... Grossbank.' The press pack stop writing and look up. They glance at me, then at Sir Oliver, who stares implacably ahead. As if he could give a shit. He's done his deal. Some of them can't resist smirking. 'You will be aware that in many instances when two investment banking businesses are merged, the firms involved appoint co-heads of divisions, one from each firm, drawing on the experience and expertise of both sides to ensure a smooth and orderly transition.' Heads are nodding sagely in the audience. Behind me on the big screen, two organograms appear side by side. One is the Bartons management structure, with the names of its heads of Equities, Corporate Finance, Fixed Income, Structured Finance and so on. Beside it is the equivalent for Grossbank. As I push a button, the two merge into one, but in each case only one name is left on the screen: the name of the Grossbank head of department. 'We aren't doing that. We believe it's wasteful, lacking in clarity, and simply postpones the inevitable. We don't shy away from tough decisions.' Like the decision to fire the other firm's people and keep the devils I know. I can hear tittering in the audience. 'I'm going to hand over now to Sir Oliver, who will say a few words from Bartons' side.'

Sir Oliver clears his throat and looks around the audience. 'Thank you, Dave. Ladies and gentlemen, today is a great day. It represents the culmination of many years' hard work, and the crystallisation of a vision that I have long cherished. No one could be more delighted than me today. For me this is the pinnacle of my career, and I shall be retiring shortly from banking a very happy man, knowing that my legacy is in safe hands. I'd like to pay particular tribute to two people who have worked harder than any others to make this happen.' He points to Rory, still standing by the stage looking awkward. 'Most of you know Rory, who has been my right hand here for many years. Rory is to become Deputy Chairman of Grossbank London, working directly for Dave Hart, much as he has been today. This underlines Grossbank's commitment to maintaining the culture and traditions of Bartons.' Rory knew nothing of this, but I'd swear I can see the colour draining from his face. Yes, pal, grease up, bend over, grasp your ankles and say stick it in and make it hurt. Every day from now until you finally give up and quit. Revenge, as they say in Spain, is a dish best eaten cold. 'And of course I have to thank Dave Hart.' He turns to me and we shake hands for the cameras with great beaming smiles on our faces. 'Thank you, Dave, from the bottom of my heart.' He leans away from the microphone and growls into my ear, 'And from my wallet...'

\*       \*       \*

THE MONDAY morning directors' meeting at Bartons used to terrify me. We called it morning prayers, mainly because we needed to pray for those whom Rory would prey upon. We used to sit at an oval conference table and try to justify our presence on the team, bragging about all the deals we were planning, the chairmen and chief executives we were pitching to, and the revenues that would surely come our way. It was almost entirely bullshit, and it bred a climate of dishonesty, lies and fear, which I guess is what Rory wanted.

So this Monday I thought I'd join him round at Bartons for the first morning prayer meeting since the announcement – to encourage the troops. I'm bringing with me two colleagues from Grossbank: Werner Grubmann, who still hasn't learnt to brush his teeth, and

Dieter Kuntz, who is a new addition to my personal hit squad of stormtroopers.

Dieter Kuntz not only has a great name, but is physically huge, close to seven feet tall, broad shouldered and heavily overweight, with almost unnaturally huge hands, and large, coarse, pale features. His fingers are so fat that he can't use a normal keyboard, and when he clutches a pen it looks like a toothpick in his hand. I call him the Mountain Troll. I don't actually know what his skill-set is, but as soon as I spotted him, I had him seconded to London with a big pay rise. He barely speaks English, which is fine, because he has a deep, guttural, booming voice that seems to get him what he wants without actually mastering the relevant language. He's a natural for my team, and his first assignment is Bartons. They'll love him.

We arrive early, and sit at the head of the table with Rory. It doesn't normally work like this. Usually the troops assemble, chat among themselves, exchange a little banter, and then Rory arrives when he's ready. Today their faces tell the story as they arrive, smiles disappear and they glance anxiously at their watches. No, they aren't late. Rory and the new owners are early.

The faces are different from my time – investment bankers are a pretty mobile bunch, moving from firm to firm before their bad deals catch up with them, leaving as soon as their two year guaranteed bonus periods expire to sign on somewhere else on what they hope will be better terms.

There are twelve men and three women, which seems pretty enlightened by City standards, but then I realise that one of the women is a secretary who is taking the minutes and another is there to pour the coffee.

Rory clears his throat. 'Good morning. I'd like to introduce…'

'Don't bother.' I cut across him before he can finish his sentence. 'I think everybody knows me.' A deathly hush descends. I like deathly hushes. They're wondering if I'm about to hand out black bin-liners. They really have no idea. That would be far too quick.

Rory looks flustered. This is his territory, and he wants to re-assert himself. 'Dave, perhaps we could go round the table and the team could introduce themselves and say a few words…'

'Nah.' I cut him off with a wave of my hand. There's a long silence. I stare around the room, looking at each of them in turn. I like long silences even more than deathly hushes. Silences can be hugely productive. They give me the chance to work out who these people are. I spot the nervous ones, the no-hopers, the arrogant ones who couldn't give a damn, and even one who seems to find it all slightly amusing – probably already has an offer from another firm.

I clear my throat. 'Let me introduce two colleagues from Grossbank, Doktor Grubmann, on my left, and Doktor Kuntz on my right. They are going to assess the department's work, its key client relationships, its skills, experience and track record, and then…' I pause and look around the table again, '…and then they'll make recommendations.' I turn to the Mountain Troll, beside whom Rory looks like a primary schoolboy. 'Doktor Kuntz, would you care to make a few remarks?'

Kuntz has barely understood a word I've said, but Werner has briefed him on what to do next. In his deep, booming, growling voice he launches into a twenty minute speech – all of it in German – that varies between the purely aggressive and the completely totalitarian, punctuated by periodic arm waving and fist-smashing on the conference room table to illustrate a point, while Rory and the team stare in disbelief. It's 1940 all over again, only without the RAF.

When he finally finishes, I turn to him and nod my appreciation. 'Thank you, Doktor Kuntz. I think that concludes the welcoming remarks.'

Christ, I love my job.

\*       \*       \*

THERE IS a postscript, about three months later.

I stand watching lines of sad faces trooping out of the Bartons building. They are all carrying black bin-liners with their personal possessions, having cleared out their desks. Nice, discreet black bin-liners of the sort favoured by Human Resources people when they get to have their fifteen seconds of glory and finally nail the arrogant hot shots who have never respected them, and whom they are finally making redundant. 'Here, take a black bin-liner and clear out your desk. Then off you go, out into the street. No one will notice. We all carry black bin-liners these days.'

When the last person leaves the building, around eight o'clock at night, I'm filmed standing in front of the main entrance, as someone flicks a switch and the lights go out all over the building. It's a moment of great symbolism. A hundred and fifty years of British banking tradition. London's last chance at a home-grown global investment banking player. Stripped of its capital, all I kept was the investment management business that was housed elsewhere. The investment banking business has been written down to nothing in what some in the press have unhelpfully called a scorched earth policy.

It's a poignant moment, and I put a handkerchief to my cheek for the cameras, then – yeehaa! – off to celebrate in the private dining room at Colon, the in-place on the King's Road, Chelsea, with Erica from Amsterdam and Eva from Hamburg.

A few months later I'll be back, in the early hours of a Saturday morning, when the City is more or less empty, the whole area cordoned off, and the building swathed in thick plastic sheeting to prevent glass or debris dispersing around the area. That's when I get to press the button.

We all have our demons to slay.

Me especially.

*     *     *

I'M WALKING down the King's Road, after paying my semi-annual visit to the flat off Sloane Square where Wendy, my avaricious ex-wife, lives with Samantha, our daughter and her meal ticket.

By my rough calculation the visit has cost me about £300,000 – about half a peanut based on my last year's compensation, but I'm not going to tell Wendy that. It needn't have cost even this much, but I was always a soft touch, and I definitely don't want Wendy and her lawyers finding out how much I'm making. Besides, it's easier to write a cheque than actually do the whole 'quality time' thing. Or maybe I'm just lazier than I am greedy.

Anyway, Wendy obviously needs holidays in Verbier (Christmas), Klosters (February half-term), the Seychelles (Easter) and Tuscany (the school summer vacation) so that Samantha can learn to ski, swim, sail, ride, etc. And now that Samantha is four, Wendy needs more help in the flat, so a second housekeeper is going on the payroll, along with various part-time tutors, and of course she really ought to have her own driver. Then there's the question of air travel. What with all the security scares, she has to take Samantha by private jet, and so on and so forth. After an hour of this, feeling irritated and vaguely bored, I need a break and some fresh air.

Tom is driving the Merc slowly along the pavement beside me, the Range Rovers are in convoy, and the Meat Factory are with me, Scary Andy on my left and Arnie the Terminator on my right, with the rest of the team around us. It's a sunny day and we're all wearing sunglasses to go with our suits and ties. It could be a scene straight from Reservoir Dogs.

Anywhere else in the world we'd get curious looks, but this is the King's Road, Chelsea, and most of the people who live around here are just like me – they live in their own social exclusion zone. If a stranger isn't famous or useful, they ignore him.

As we amble slowly along, we come to a series of pavement cafes. At the first one, a pretty young woman with strawberry blonde hair is trying to negotiate a path for her pushchair between the tables. She's slim, with small breasts and she's wearing a short denim skirt and a simple t-shirt. There's a weedy management consultant type dressed in new media black, even down to his collarless shirt and dark glasses, sitting alone at a table, tapping into one of those neat, rinky-dink little laptops that people like that can never be without, and he's blocking her path. Naturally, he carries on tapping, pausing only to sip his decaf espresso. Jerk. It gets worse. A waiter appears and waves to her. 'No, madam. You can't come in here with the pushchair. We don't have room. You'll have to collapse it.'

He's an olive-skinned, vaguely handsome garlic belt European with a slightly dodgy accent and he really pisses me off.

I stop. We all stop. The Meat Factory follow my glance and stare at the waiter. I really don't give a shit about the stupid woman and her pushchair, but it pisses me off when people piss me off. I remove my sunglasses and step forward so that I'm standing in front of the waiter and he can't ignore me. I pause and look him in the eye, saying nothing. He looks uncertain. His uncertainty visibly increases when Arnie and Scary Andy step forward and stand on either side of me. I lean close to him, so close that he probably thinks I'm going to kiss him. The woman has stopped trying to get her pushchair past the management consultant and is watching what is going on. I whisper in the waiter's ear.

'Why don't you go fold some napkins?'

It's a wonderful moment. The Sopranos meet the King's Road, Chelsea. Guess who blinks first. As the waiter scurries off to the back of the café, I hear the door of the Merc slam and Tom appears beside me.

I nod towards the management consultant, who is tapping into his little machine just a bit too studiously.

'Tom, could you help this gentleman to get out of the lady's way?'

Tom bends down and grasps the man's chair on either side, and lifts it – and him – up into the air and places them on top of the table. The guy shouts 'Hey, what are you doing?' in a terrified, squeaky sort of voice, and hangs onto his laptop and the edge of the chair. Then he's no longer sitting at the table, but on it. Strange how a few extra feet of elevation can change a man from Cool to Pratt. A couple of Sloane Ranger types walk past and laugh. I nod in their direction. 'Installation art.' This cracks them up even more.

The woman with the pushchair has decided it's best to leave. I pass Tom a wad of notes. 'See if you can get the lady a table at the place next door.'

She's not sure how to respond. 'It's all right, actually I...'

'I insist. You shouldn't have to put up with crap like that. Let me buy you a coffee.' I give her what I hope is a dazzling smile. She's actually quite pretty, with definite possibilities. I look down at the child in the pushchair. 'And what's your name?'

The woman is flustered, unsure whether to get the hell out of Dodge or be charmed. 'Her name's Ruth. She's nearly two.'

'Fantastic age. Come on, let's go next door and have that coffee. I'm gasping for one. My name's Dave, by the way, Dave Hart.'

'I'm Paula. Paula Hayes.' We shake hands, and she has

a delightfully powerful grip. I'm a sucker for a woman with a firm grip.

We leave the dork to climb down by himself and go next door for a coffee. Christ, I'm nice. If I was this nice all the time, even I might start to like me. I ask more about the baby, and coo and gurgle at her, and I ask about Paula, what she does (nothing, she lives in Chelsea), where in Chelsea she lives (just off Sloane Avenue) and finally, having spotted her wedding ring, what her husband does.

'Sean's a banker.'

'Really? Small world. I'm in banking too. What area does he work in?'

'Syndicated loans. Please don't ask me to explain. I have no idea what it is he actually does.'

'Syndicated loans? You're kidding – is that *the* Sean Hayes?' She shrugs, embarrassed, not sure how to respond. Actually I've never heard of Sean Hayes, and have no interest at all in syndicated loans. But I am interested in her. I reach into my jacket pocket and pull out a business card, which I slide across the table. 'I run Grossbank in London, Sean will have heard of me. We're desperate to hire a new head of syndicated loans.' At least we will be as soon as I get into the office and fire whoever it is who runs syndicated loans at the moment. 'We're paying top dollar.' She reaches out to pick up the card and I place my hand on hers. 'You will promise to get him to call me, won't you?' She blushes and gently pulls her hand away.

'Yes, I will.'

I smile and lean forward, looking her straight in the eye. 'You see? We were meant to meet.'

Awesome. I try to imagine her face when she's having an orgasm. I always do this with women. I think she'd be a screamer, or at least she would be once I'd had my way with her.

I signal the waitress to come over. 'Check, please.'

The waitress is late teens, Eastern European, slightly dumpy with a spotty complexion. No possibilities *there*. I hold out my Grossbank corporate Amex card, and she plugs it into a portable credit card reader.

'Two coffees, nine pounds fifty pence.'

I tap my PIN number into the machine, and when it prompts me to give a tip, I tap in ten thousand pounds, press Enter and hand it back to the waitress. She's pressed the button and a receipt is printing out before she realises what I've done.

'I'm sorry, sir, I think there is some mistake.'

I shake my head. 'No mistake, just one condition.'

'One condition?' She looks dubious. I look her up and down. Nah, she must be kidding.

'The condition is that you show it to the wanker who runs the place next door.'

Beside me, Paula Hayes can't stop laughing.

\*　　　\*　　　\*

I'M SITTING in traffic on Piccadilly, my little convoy half way to the bank, caught in another snarl-up that just goes to show how ineffective the congestion charge has been in clearing the riff-raff off the streets of London. It may surprise you to know that I'm a huge supporter of the Green agenda. I want road pricing, congestion charging and higher petrol prices, and all as soon as possible. Drive the poor off the roads. Motoring should be the privilege of the rich. And as for air travel, even more so. Half the problem at airports is all the tourists going on holiday, the vast fungible masses moving around the world, taking their lager swilling, fish-and-chip habits to ruin beautiful places. Why can't they just stay at home and lie on the sofa watching day-time TV, ThickTalk with Jessy Swinger, or the latest reality zoo-show?

By the time I get to the bank I'm in a foul mood.

I'm worried that some people are starting to think I'm nuts. Or maybe I just think they do. Maybe I'm paranoid. It could be the drugs. And I think I'm getting predictable. In investment banking, predictable is dangerous. It means you're losing your edge. The other day I was chairing a Management Committee – I had nothing better to do – and we were discussing what to do with operations staff who have been at Grossbank for twenty-five years. Fire them, I hear you say, but you're wrong. Back office staff who stay in one place are good news. They give you continuity while all the hot shot front office revenue-generators come and go through the revolving doors.

Anyway, someone suggested we give them classy watches – Rolex or Patek, say – and someone else suggested we send them on holiday with their wives – a couple of weeks in a villa in Spain. Can you believe that I'm dealing with this stuff? Such is the burden of leadership.

Anyway, I said bullshit, we should hire a stretch limo full of hookers and champagne and send them off for a night on the town. At least they'd remember it – well, maybe. Paul Ryan objected.

'Come on, Dave, we can't do that. We're a respectable firm.'

I looked at him and replied, 'Yes we can. We're Grossbank, and we can do anything.' And do you know what? They all mouthed the words in time with me. Predictable, or what?

If I don't re-invent myself soon, I'm toast.

Today I'm due to be briefed by some young guys who are working on a pitch for a major piece of business in the Middle East. We want to win the mandate for the stock market flotation of a state-owned oil producer controlled by the Sultan of Dahar. I'm doing this one personally, to show the bank's commitment to the business. Or at least I'll be wheeled in to perform some ceremonial, and with any luck as the Senior Resource on the deal, I won't blow it – what investment bankers call a 'blue on blue' – by getting the name of the company wrong or thinking it's a hotel business or a ball-bearing manufacturer.

The team are led by one of our young Turks, a Brit called Mike Hanlan, only five years out of university – a Cambridge rowing blue – and are all high-testosterone, pumped-up types except for a bookish, young woman with glasses, short sandy hair and freckles, who looks like she should be a librarian rather than an investment banker. Even sitting down she's very tall – I guess over six feet – and somehow looks out of place with the guys. She's slightly stooped, the way tall people sometimes are when they are too conscious of their height. There's an undercurrent of tension in the room as I come in. We run through the presentation, I make appropriate noises, and she says very little, though whenever there's some additional follow-up work to do, it seems to get pushed her way. When we're done, I push back my chair and stare at them.

'Good effort, guys, but you've forgotten one thing.'

Hanlan's immediately on the defensive. 'What's that?'

'The human element.'

Still they look dumbly back at me.

'The Sultan's got notorious… appetites.'

'Appetites?'

I nod and gaze across at the librarian. I bet she doesn't get laid that often. Maybe not at all. 'When he comes over to London for the presentations, he's going to want… entertaining. That's where we have an opportunity to distinguish ourselves from the competition.' I stare at her, poker-faced.

She blushes and the others nudge each other and try not to laugh. Finally she takes a deep breath and fixes me with an icy stare. I like her more this way. At least she has guts. 'Exactly what sort of entertainment do you have in mind, Mister Hart?'

I look straight back at her, equally icy. 'Whatever it takes.' I turn and look at the guys. 'We do this for the firm.' They are nodding their agreement now, enjoying this unexpected turn of events. 'We're committed.' I turn to Hanlan. 'Aren't we, Mike?'

He gives an emphatic 'Yes, sir.'

'We want to win and we'll go the extra mile – or more…'

She looks as if she's about to burst into tears. I put on a puzzled look.

'You seem upset. What's the problem?'

Far from crying, she's bursting with anger. I like her more and more. 'Mister Hart, I will not be used as some piece of corporate meat for the sake of winning this or any other business.'

Hanlan can't resist. 'But it's for the firm. Think of the fees, the bonus…'

I nod my agreement. 'Exactly. And besides, it's not as if it's you who's being asked to make the sacrifice.'

She looks up, puzzled.

'The Sultan's gay. It's Mike here who'll be going the extra mile.' I get up, smiling, and slap Hanlan on the shoulder. 'Way to go, Mike. I'll let you know when and where you're needed.'

He's staring at me, suddenly rather pale. I turn to the others. 'We may need more of you than just Mike. Depends what the Sultan wants on the night. I'll find out and let you know. Think of yourselves as Team Harem, and remember, you're doing this for Grossbank. Think of the bonus, guys.'

I leave the room with an unaccustomed spring in my step. Christ, I'm good. The only question now is whether to get Dan Harriman to black up and tie a sheet around his head in a hotel suite in Mayfair, so we can film Mike and the guys doing the dance of the seven veils for the Christmas party.

\*     \*     \*

HERMAN LOVES me. 'Herman the German' recently celebrated his 50th birthday, and he is by far the youngest Chairman ever of Grossbank. He is slim, trim, works out daily, dresses snappily, and has a pretty wife and a young family. Apparently he even goes to church. He's been my biggest supporter at Grossbank, flying air cover whenever I stuck my neck out, defending me against the politics of the fossils on the board, who would have stopped the investment banking initiative that has turned into its main profit driver. I've often told him that he and I are joined at the hip. Well, the wallet anyway.

Naturally enough, in the finest traditions of investment banking, as the next step in my inevitable career progression, I'm going to knife him. I think he rather likes the idea of me joining him on the main board of the bank, which would be a first for a non-German. What he doesn't have in mind is that I should join the board as Chairman.

I could be patient, wait my turn, serve my time, be a good corporate trooper and eventually prosper. Or I could go for it now. Guess which I'm going to do. I don't believe in patience, and I don't believe in give and take. I believe in take and take. Preferably immediately.

In order to help me raise my profile in Germany, Herman has suggested that I make a major policy announcement on behalf of the bank at the annual assembly of German University business and finance students. In the past this has been a bit of a poisoned chalice. Big business leaders have been invited to give keynote speeches in front of up to five thousand students, only to be heckled, sprayed with paint, hit with eggs, and all the other fun stuff that spoilt radical children do before they grow up. This year it's taking place at the University of Freiburg, in the so-called Auditorium Maximum, or AudiMax, and the place will be packed.

The initiative that Herman wants me to announce is that the board have decided to set up the Grossbank Foundation. The Foundation will receive one per cent of the net profits of the bank, to be used to build up an endowment fund to support charitable causes not just in Germany but everywhere the bank operates. In these days of corporate social responsibility, the bank is going to do its bit. And if one per cent doesn't sound like much, it is a multiple of what most financial services firms give to good causes (unlike the bonus pool, which is the ultimate good cause, and which typically gets ten to fifteen per cent).

Freiburg is a picturesque town in the Southwest corner of Germany, near to where Germany, France and Switzerland meet, and it has a convenient airfield just big enough to take a Grossbank private jet, which Two Livers and I fly out in with a couple of bodyguards on the Saturday afternoon before my speech.

We are met by the local branch manager, who has cars waiting to take us to our hotel. He wants to take us to dinner, but I explain that I'm tired and need to rehearse my speech, and if he doesn't mind, I'd appreciate an early night. As soon as he's gone, I get out my little black book, make a couple of calls, and leave Two Livers in the hotel bar, claiming I'm going to get my head down. Which in a manner of speaking I am.

It is only the next morning, Sunday, when the hammering on the door of my hotel room finally wakes me, that I wonder if it was an indulgence too far. As I struggle to open my eyes, I can hear the sound of people moaning and sighing, at least one man and several women. It's typical of the fake pleasure sounds I associate with the kind of nights I'm used to having on these trips. But then I freak out – it's morning, and who the hell is having sex in my room? I open my eyes. Phew. It's the Pay TV. I must have left the porn channel on full volume all night. I wonder what the people in the neighbouring rooms made of it. They probably think I'm a stud, which of course I am, though not to that extent. But what about the people banging on the door now?

I look around. The real girls have gone, but there are empty bottles scattered around my suite, and traces of white powder on the dressing table and the bedside cabinet. Shit.

I look at myself in the mirror. My eyes are bloodshot, my hands are shaking and I have dark circles round my eyes. Even my crow's feet have crow's feet. Why didn't I press my Stop button? I think I know the answer to that one. I don't have a Stop button. At least that's what I keep telling myself, so it isn't my fault. I'm a victim too. I look about ten years older than the normal ten years older than my actual age which I generally look. I try to speak, to ask who is at the door, but my mouth is dry and tastes horrible.

I flick the remote control and silence the mega sex scene on the TV screen.

'Dave, open up. It's me.' It's Two Livers. Damn. 'I'm here with Doktor Heinze.' Heinze's the branch manager. He's not a real doctor, just a nerd with a PhD, so he won't be much use. 'It's time we left for the conference.'

I need to do something fast, otherwise the bodyguards will kick the door down to see what's happening. I close my eyes, take a few deep breaths to fight back a wave of nausea, and yell back, 'Give me ten minutes. I'll see you downstairs.'

I've been here before, and have a pretty good routine. First an ice cold shower that gets my heart racing, and one day might actually kill me, but in the meantime wakes me up and partially clears my head. Teeth, shave and dress, and twenty minutes later I join them in the lobby, where Heinze is fretting that we're going to be late.

Two Livers knows at once. She sends Heinze out to the car and takes me on one side. 'Dave, what did you do last night?'

I'm wearing sunglasses to hide my eyes. 'Not enough. If I had I'd still be flying. I feel like shit.'

'You look like shit. You going to be able to keep it together?'

I take off my sunglasses and give her a sideways look. She winces. 'When have I ever let you down?'

*   *   *

IT'S ELEVEN o'clock on Sunday morning and the AudiMax lecture theatre is full with the conference delegates, mostly students and academics from all over Germany, but with a sprinkling of government ministers and business leader types, and of course the press. I don't know quite what the building's capacity is, but thousands of not particularly welcoming faces are staring at me as I ascend to the podium. Where do these kids come from? They have beards and long hair, and wear blue jeans and T-shirts. Has nobody told them the sixties are over?

Two Livers and I are seated with the other panel members at the back of the stage, looking out at the audience. I'm clutching my speech, which I still haven't read, because my head is spinning and I keep getting hit by waves of nausea. I have a horrible feeling I'm going to throw up mid-way through. I'm sweating profusely, my shirt is sticking to my back beneath my jacket, and I keep wiping my face with my handkerchief. I definitely overdid it last night. I feel as if every pore of my body is oozing a toxic mixture of alcohol, cocaine and Viagra. I imagine it being sucked up into the air conditioning and circulated around the conference room among the delegates. Christ. This audience is bad enough already.

I'm introduced by a grey-haired professor of economics, and as I sway towards the lectern I drop a handful of papers. Fuck it, I toss the lot away. Two Livers looks worried – she's been there before when I go off message – but all I'm focussing on is getting to the lectern and grabbing hold of it with both hands so I can keep myself upright.

There's some desultory applause, then silence. I look around the hall. Oh, fuck, now I have to say something. Why am I here?

'Focus.' Who said that? It was me. Damn. I didn't mean to say it out loud. Deep breath. 'Distinguished professors, ministers, ladies and gentlemen – focus is the new word in banking.' In the front row, some of the beardos are yawning ostentatiously, nudging each other. 'Focus not only on our core business, but on our core values. What do we stand for as a firm?' If only I knew. The beardos are definitely twitching. Stand by for a slow hand clap. In my mind's eye some numbers are floating around in the air. There's something I have to announce, but I'm suddenly so tired, so profoundly, utterly, deeply fatigued in a way that only an all night orgy or running six marathons can achieve. I feel as if I could fall asleep standing up. Would anyone notice? Probably – this isn't one of those dull, academic conferences where people nod politely and the audience quietly dozes off. This is more like the Roman arena. These guys want blood. If only I had an idiot board in front of me as a prompt. Another deep breath. 'That's why today I have a major announcement to make on behalf of Grossbank. An announcement that will help shape the future course not only of our business, but of the communities in which we operate.' Some of it's coming back to me now. It's just the figures I can't remember. 'Yes, Grossbank is big business. But big business can have a heart as well as a head. And big business can give back to society as well as drawing benefit from it.' One point zero comes to mind, or is it zero point one? Or one and zero? 'I'm proud to announce the establishment of a new Foundation, the Grossbank Foundation, that will manage a major new endowment fund supporting charitable and social causes both in Germany and throughout the world. The bank will fund this new Foundation by contributing a portion of its net profits each year.' The beardos are getting ready for something. It must be an ambush. I can see things being passed from hand to hand in the first couple of rows. Eggs? Tomatoes? Paint bombs? 'That percentage will be...' Think, Hart, think. Oh, damn. If in doubt, go large. '...ten per cent of all net profits of Grossbank worldwide. We'll be doing this with immediate effect, and we're doing it because we want to change the world we live and work in. For our own sake, and for our children.'

There's a stunned silence in the room. Everyone is looking at me. The professors, the panellists on the podium, Two Livers, even the beardos, are all open-mouthed. I glance down to check my flies aren't undone. What have I said? All I want to do is get off this podium, run to the men's room and throw up. Never again will I mix drink and drugs and hookers the night before a major speech. Well, not unless I'm really bored.

And then the applause starts. I look up and the beardos are all standing, and they are shouting at the tops of their voices, clapping and cheering like they want to raise the roof, and then some of them start chanting, 'GROSSBANK... GROSSBANK... GROSSBANK...'

The grey-haired economics professor wants them to quieten down, but they won't, so I take it as my cue to leave, waving to the audience, manage to step down from the podium without falling over, and Two Livers takes me by the arm and helps me out to the car, where she tells the driver to get us to the airport as fast as he can.

Only when I'm sitting in the car and we've put a full ten minutes between us and the conference hall does she turn to me, still shaking her head, eyes full of disbelief.

'Christ, Dave, what have you done?'

I turn to her and try to work out what's going on. My brain still isn't fully engaged. 'I've no idea. What have I done?'

*       *       *

'DON'T YOU know the difference between one point zero and ten? There is a small matter of a decimal point. What kind of banker are you?' It's a good question. Herman is shouting so loud the words are distorted on the speakerphone. Two Livers and I are back in the office in London, and there's a full scale crisis underway.

I've goofed. Sure, Grossbank wanted to be generous, and one per cent was huge compared to most firms, but ten per cent is ridiculous. It's Sunday night, and the board has been assembled in Germany to work out what to do next. The news of Grossbank's initiative has shocked the worldwide business community. The impact on shareholders – and therefore the share price – is too awful to contemplate. When our shares start trading again tomorrow, the world believes they will go into free-fall. So do I. No business can give so much of its profits away and not expect the market to react. And who do we think we are, anyway? Our job is to make profits, to pay dividends to shareholders. We're a business, not a charity.

The problem is, the announcement has been made, and the board are too afraid to issue a correction: 'What Mister Hart really meant was...' It is particularly difficult in Germany, where many liberal commentators think this is a fantastic development, that finally a major financial institution is doing the right thing, making the right social commitment, showing the rest a fine example. So the board are like a rabbit caught in the headlights, and the only thing they know for sure is that this is my fault, and as soon as the noise dies down, I'm toast.

I do the only thing a man can do on an occasion like

this, and call the Silver Fox. We – or at least I – have to have a strategy. I've got twelve hours to work out what to do, and how to dig myself out. For once I'm not bored.

He takes about half an hour to come to the office – he is always dining at some smart restaurant or other in the evenings, usually with a newly divorced or separated actress or model on his arm, but tonight when he arrives, he has a whole team with him: branding consultants, advertising people, speechwriters, you name it, he has them. They set up camp in some of the Grossbank meeting rooms, and I take him into my office.

'Dave, this is about you. You are the story here...'

I hold up my hands to stop him before he goes any further. 'You don't have to win this business. It's yours already, whatever the cost.' I look at him imploringly. 'Just save me...'

\*　　　\*　　　\*

OUR STOCK closed Friday at seventy-five euros a share. On Monday morning the Frankfurt market opens and Grossbank shares are off ten per cent within minutes of the start of dealings. Not only are institutional investors bailing out of a stock that clearly can't pay the sort of dividends the other German banks can – because they aren't so dumb as to give away ten per cent of their profits to charity – but the hedge funds are shorting the hell out of Grossbank, opportunistically trying to drive us even further underwater, selling shares they don't own, but have borrowed from elsewhere at seventy-five euros, hoping to buy them back in a few weeks at fifty, netting a fat profit out of our misery. Our share price hits sixty euros, it is the big story of the week, and some of the institutional shareholders are actually asking if the board will re-consider their decision on the Grossbank Foundation. Re-consider it? Hell, yes – they didn't even make it. They'd love to re-consider.

At eleven o'clock, having been carefully coached by the Silver Fox, I fire my first salvo. I do a live interview for EuroBizTv, a satellite business channel carried all over the world, and syndicated to most of the German TV stations.

I do it from the trading floor at Grossbank in London, where a pretty woman reporter, a camera man and a sound guy have been prepped by the Silver Fox.

'Mister Hart – what is your reaction to the fall in the Grossbank share price? Is giving to charity bad for business?'

Relaxed smile. 'Absolutely not. If there are people out there who are uncomfortable with our business philosophy, I'd rather they didn't own our shares. We're taking a moral stand here, and that's what matters to me.'

'Even if your shares keep on falling?'

'You can't run a business of the scale of Grossbank – or any of the major German banks – and spend your life worrying about daily share price movements. We're here for the long term, and people need to know where we stand. Grossbank is different from the other German banks, and proud to be so.'

'How is Grossbank different?'

'None of our competitors has given anything like the commitment that we have to putting something back into society. By banking with us, our customers are making a moral statement. They are saying we want to do business with a firm that believes in our moral values, that is prepared to sacrifice profit for the future benefit of society, for our children and our children's children. That's the difference.'

'But do customers care?'

'We'll see. It's easy to say you believe in moral values, but people need to demonstrate commitment, as we have done. If there are people listening to this interview in Germany, who bank elsewhere, they should think about that. Do they want to bank with a firm that doesn't care, or one that does? It's their choice.'

'Dave Hart, head of investment banking at Grossbank, London, thank you...'

I do a whole series of similar interviews for the print media, a couple for radio, and some pre-records for late night business TV shows in Germany. Meanwhile our stock's hit fifty euros. I call the Silver Fox, who says to stay calm. We've done all we can for today, tomorrow will be the acid test.

As I know I won't sleep anyway, I call the Pussy-Cat Club and book Fluffy and Thumper in the private room...

\*       \*       \*

THE NEXT day starts early, even by City standards. I get a text message from the Silver Fox – 'It's started'. What's started? I'm early in the office and stay glued to one of the big TV screens on the trading floor. They are showing scenes from Freiburg, where I first gave the speech that started all this. There are lines of mostly young people outside the main Grossbank branch, waiting for it to open. Some of them are interviewed and explain how they are moving their accounts from other banks to Grossbank. Later they show other places. To begin with, it is particularly strong in university towns where there are lots of young people, but in the course of the day it starts to catch fire across the whole country. In no time Grossbank's branch network is being overwhelmed by new account openings, and the internet banking site goes down under the volume of hits. The share price carries on falling for a time, then stabilises around forty-five euros. The business news channels carry interviews with hard-nosed analysts – twenty-five year olds who know nothing about anything – trying to work out whether increased market share might cancel out the negative effect of giving away ten per cent of profits. The prevailing view is that it won't, and the stock starts to fall again.

The next couple of days are hell. In Germany, we've signed over three million new customers, but are losing momentum because the system simply cannot cope. The board are reserving their judgement and I stop getting calls from Herman. Now we fire the second salvo: a full-blown advertising campaign with some big shot TV stars, singers and comedians, saying on German TV, 'I'm with Grossbank. Are you?' The logo for the campaign is a thumbs up sign, and we're printing millions of bumper stickers, badges and baseball caps. We want to create the New Cool, and the Silver Fox is masterminding a viral marketing campaign starting in the universities. By the end of the week, we've passed the five million new account openings mark, the system is in meltdown, and the stock is hovering just above forty euros a share. As we head into the weekend, we need to pull another rabbit out of the hat.

Luckily for me, that's exactly what the Silver Fox does.

Late on Sunday evening, I do another interview, this time in a TV studio in Frankfurt, with a leading German business commentator.

'Mister Hart, the Grossbank campaign has attracted over five million new account holders for your bank in a single week, but it still has not stopped your share price falling to a little more than forty euros a share. It has almost halved since you announced this new initiative. How can you say it has been a success?'

'The Grossbank share price has been manipulated downwards. It's being sold short artificially by mostly foreign institutions – hedge funds and speculators. These people have no understanding of business, let alone morality. For them this is all about short-term profit. And you're right, what they've done has been to force our share price down to little more than half the level of a week ago. But that's good news.'

'Good news? I don't think your shareholders would agree, Mister Hart.'

'Right now, perhaps not. But when the benefit of five million new account holders works through to profits, there'll be a different story. And in the meantime, the share price at such an artificially low level presents a huge opportunity.'

'How so?'

'Anyone who believes in Grossbank and what it's doing should buy our shares. They've been forced down to this level by international manipulators and at forty euros they are a bargain. The people who voted with their feet by moving bank accounts should buy our shares too. Buy one share, buy two or three or five or whatever you can afford. Buy them for yourself, for your children or your grandchildren. Because you're investing in an institution that will change the way business is done. This is not for now, it's for the future. For all of our futures.'

In fact, the particular future I have uppermost in my mind is my own, but I say all this with my best 'earnest conviction' look, head tilted sympathetically to one side, leaning forward into the camera, smiling, relaxed and positive. Out of camera shot, the Silver Fox gives me a double thumbs-up.

I've done my bit, now we need to see what tomorrow brings. I leave the Silver Fox in the studio chatting to the presenter and head back to my hotel room to ponder my future with Inge, twenty-three, from Cologne, and Iona, twenty-one, from Athens. I try not to think too much about what will happen next.

*         *         *

TWICE IN the twentieth century the world learnt to tremble when the Germans went on tour. On Monday morning they do it again, only this time they do it peacefully.

From the trading floor at Grossbank in London, Paul Ryan is giving me a running commentary. 'Massive retail buying, there's been more volume in the first hour of trading than in the whole of Friday. Millions of individual orders. The Exchange are saying the shares may have to be suspended if it continues. They're already close to capacity and the system could crash.'

'But where are we on price?' I'm still in my hotel near the Grossbank Tower in Frankfurt, preferring not to show my face to the board until I know what's happening.

'So far, we're up two euros, hovering around the forty-three level. The hedgies are doubling up, going for quits, and some of the prop desks at the other banks are having a swing at us too.' Damn. The proprietary trading teams at the major investment banks are effectively powerful hedge funds in their own right, swinging their firms' capital around and sometimes moving markets regardless of what actual investors are doing. Soulless bastards, turning on one of their own – not that I wouldn't do the same, of course.

'What's the outlook?'

'Sorry to say it, but it's not good, boss.'

Damn. I'm sending millions of foot soldiers over the top, ordinary Germans who are putting their savings where their mouths are and taking on the hedge funds and the prop desks. But these are the big battalions of the finance world and they are mowing my guys down like the first day of the Somme. Not that I could give a shit, but if it doesn't work then it could be a disaster. I could lose my job, and that would be serious. I could be history. I watch as our share price starts to fall again, dropping through the forty-two level, and then through forty-one. I've only card left to play. I call Two Livers.

'I need a favour.'

'Boss, you need more than that. You need the Seventh Cavalry.'

'I want you to call Tripod Turner.'

There's a silence at the other end of the line. Tripod Turner and Two Livers were close once upon a time. He's the London-based Chief Investment Officer of the Boston International Group, the world's largest investing institution. Physically massive, he's said to be the biggest swinging dick of all – hence the nickname – and we are sort of buddies, though not in the way that he and Two Livers once were. I have asked her if it's true about his alleged sheer physical size, but she discreetly looked away and pretended not to hear.

'I don't want to pressurise you, but it's now or never. We've got one shot at this. Leave it another hour and we're done.'

Still there's silence.

'Are you there? Hello?'

The line's gone dead. Damn. I misplayed that one. Should never have asked. Maybe I should call him myself. Ask for a favour. No, beg for a favour. Except that never works. Once the market knows you're desperate, you're history. Kindness is for girls.

Around mid-day I watch as the stock goes through forty euros. I turn off the TV and start drafting my resignation letter. I'm half-way through it when my cell phone goes. It's Paul Ryan.

'Boss – have you seen this? It's amazing.'

'Seen what?'

'This interview – on EuroBizTv. Get yourself in front of a screen right now. It's Tripod Turner!'

I flick the remote control and sure enough, there is the big man, sitting scratching himself in his office, tie undone, shirt sleeves rolled up, bright red braces with golden dollar signs and the initials 'B.I.G.' on them.

'...and we perceive it as a major, indeed a permanent shift in the banking landscape, not just in Europe, but globally. Banks will have to do business differently in future. And Grossbank is leading the way. In the long run, we see it as very positive for Grossbank's earnings and overall positioning. That's why we're moving to a heavily overweight position in their stock, while selling off others.'

I half scream into the mobile. 'What's going on in the market? Are they buying?'

'Buying? They're stampeding. There's blood on the streets. It's terrible – terribly good for us, that is.'

I feel like crying. In fact between you and me, I might have done. It was only afterwards, at the post-mortem that I got the whole story.

Boston International Group – 'BIG by name, big by nature' – is a trillion dollar monster. In stock market terms, they are like an elephant: when they decide to sit down, they sit down, and you'd better not be underneath when they do.

The people who were selling Grossbank shares short at forty-five euros, hoping to buy them back at a lower price, were suddenly faced with an avalanche of buying that drove the price back up. If it went above the price at which they had sold, they were looking at a money-losing trade, so they had better buy the shares they needed as soon as they could. Only BIG was in there first, hoovering up anything that moved, and doing so in the kind of size that dwarfed the rest of the market.

Three or four of the biggest hedge funds, reacting

fastest to the change in circumstances, did the stock market equivalent of a handbrake turn. You could almost hear the screeching of brakes and the screaming of tortured tyres as people who were the biggest sellers suddenly became huge buyers.

For the retail buyers, the ordinary members of the public investing their savings, BIG's arrival was like hearing the bugles and seeing the cavalry charging over the hill.

Only BIG isn't the Seventh Cavalry. BIG is America's – and the world's – largest money manager. It's the US Marine Corps, the Sixth Fleet and the 82nd Airborne all rolled into one. By the time the market closed, our share price was back through sixty euros and heading north. By the end of the week it hit a high for the year of ninety-five. And I'm a hero.

Phew.

\*     \*     \*

THE THING about heroes is that they tend to be magnanimous in victory. Well, I'm not. Some devious, underhand individual has leaked to the press an internal Grossbank memo from a couple of weeks ago in which Herman states that the entire Grossbank Foundation fiasco is down to me, I should take responsibility, and in his view I should be sacked and the Foundation should be limited to one per cent of net profits.

He's instantly transformed into the most hated man in Germany. I don't mean just averagely disliked for a couple of days until the papers get bored and move onto something more important, like some actress's boob job or a rock star's latest divorce. This man is hated. It is not just the millions of members of the public who bought our shares – and profited handsomely – who hate him, but all those righteous individuals who want to see big business sharing more of the spoils. Wherever he turns, people are condemning him, and they want his scalp. He's the lead in all the German papers, and politicians of all parties are competing to outdo each other in the Bundestag in the strength of their public damnation of this personification of evil. Some whackos even threaten to kill him. Poor fellow. Can you imagine what it must be like?

As an honourable man, he has no alternative but to offer his resignation, which is accepted. It takes the board less than an hour to put in a call to me inviting me to consider taking his place as Chairman of Grossbank. I need less than half a second to decide to accept, but I make a show of reflecting on it over the weekend and disappear with Breathless Beth and Beate for some R&R in Cap Ferrat.

*       *       *

Putting me in charge of Grossbank is like giving whisky and car keys to a seventeen year old boy.

I arrive in Frankfurt a week later for my first board meeting, and head up to my office on the fifty-fourth floor of the Grossbank Tower. I haven't actually seen this office before, but it is suitably vast – nearly a hundred feet across – high tech, high spec, full of tasteless chrome and glass and generally excessive, resembling the headquarters of the chief villain in one of the early Bond movies.

Just to show how utterly vulgar they think I am, they've brought a Damon Hersh Elephant in Formaldehyde giant glass-tank from the bank's contemporary art collection and installed it in the office, presumably as a conversation piece, or maybe because the 'artist' and I share the same initials.

When I travel to Frankfurt for board meetings, the Meat Factory come with me, along with Maria, and of course Two Livers and Paul Ryan, as my right hands, and Rory to carry the bags. Two Livers and Paul have been promoted. They are now co-heads of global investment banking. From a practical standpoint, it makes no difference, since between them they ran investment banking anyway. I was just the boss, and always took a 'hands off' stance – at least with regard to Paul – so that they could get on with the task of making things happen, while I concentrated on not fucking things up, which I've generally felt is the best contribution most heads of investment banks can make to their teams, leaving the markets to do the rest.

I've always believed that it is easier to seek forgiveness than permission, and on that basis intend to try to change things radically from the start, taking advantage of my honeymoon period as Chairman to force things through before the Grossbank bureaucracy smothers me and the walls close in the way they do in all large organisations and ultimately institutionalise me.

The first thing I'm going to change is the board. The only detail is that they don't know it yet.

The only board member I've really known, other than Herman, is an old guy called Biedermann. When I first joined the bank, Biedermann led the opposition to the future direction of the firm, saying the investment banking strategy would waste the legacy of the bank, ruin its good name and ultimately serve only to line the pockets of the hot-shot foreigners who would come in and fleece them.

In principle, he was right, and I agreed with him, though I didn't say so at the time. What he described is what investment bankers typically do to sleepy commercial banks. But I guess I just got lucky. Or at least I hired people who got lucky. It's worked. And now Biedermann has retired, allegedly on grounds of ill health – presumably brought on by the prospect of calling me Chairman – and I'm left with a room full of ancient, fossilised strangers.

They are all seated round the board table when I arrive, and I instinctively go to the far end of the room, where I used to sit when I had to present myself to get approval for whatever nonsense I wanted to do in London.

Someone gives a meaningful cough, and I turn and see that they are all waiting for me to take my place at the head of the table.

Christ, I'm in charge. How terrifying. But it's also exhilarating. They nod respectfully and I nod back. I assume they all speak English, but just in case I keep nodding and give them all a friendly smile. It's the last bit of friendly they'll be seeing from me.

An agenda and board pack were sent to me a week ago, but I didn't bother to read them. I've got a different agenda in mind for today's meeting.

'Gentlemen, good morning.'

A few of them pick up earpieces from the table and insert them in their ears. Are they really that geriatric? No, they just don't speak English.

'First, let me say how honoured I feel to be sitting here today, and how privileged to assume such a great office. I look forward to great times ahead for the bank and for its employees and clients around the world. And of course for its shareholders.' Particularly those with senior management share option packages. 'I want this board meeting – my first – to follow a slightly unusual agenda, and propose to disregard the normal business items.'

This causes a stir. The fossils aren't accustomed to change. Probably haven't known change in decades – since they were alive in fact.

'Today I want to focus on the community that is Grossbank.' I hold my arms out wide to indicate how broad a community it is. 'Our people.'

A few of them are frowning, and one or two are tapping their earpieces and glancing at each other.

'We need to show leadership to this great organisation.' This at least they can relate to, and nod their heads in agreement. 'We need to reflect the values we claim to espouse at the highest level of the firm.' More nodding. 'There's only one way to lead, and that's from the front. Or should I say the top?' They're relaxing again now, it looks as if this is just another of those bullshit corporate values speeches.

I look down at some notes prepared for me by Paul Ryan. 'Gentlemen, do you realise that there are over seventy thousand employees working for Grossbank worldwide?'

They smile indulgently. The new kid is just getting his head around quite how big the firm is.

'Or that we have one-hundred-and-six different nationalities working for us?' They nod again. I take a deep breath and look around the room. 'But only two around this table.'

I'm expecting a long dramatic pause, but instead one of them pipes up.

'Is zat correct? My grandfather was Sviss.' It's a fossil to my right, two places down, I think his name is Hagmann and he runs the bank's business in Swabia.

'Your grandfather?'

He nods. Typical fucking Swabian. I take another deep breath.

'Okay, Doktor Hagmann, that's very helpful, thank you. Let's say two and a half. I don't really count the Swiss.' I look at my notes again. 'And the average age of our employees is thirty-five.' I stare meaningfully around the table. 'The average age in this board room is sixty-eight. It dropped significantly when I joined.' Now they are looking perplexed. What is the new boy getting at? 'And forty per cent of our employees are women. There are no women here.' Unless... no, none of these is a woman.

One of them laughs. 'But are you suggesting we should put women on the board?'

'Why not? Women are different.' I should know. 'They care. Granted, it can be a terrible weakness, but they do offer a different perspective.'

Now they're really tapping their earpieces, looking at each other, wondering what's coming next. Is it as they feared, and they've appointed a nutcase to the board? Of course not. It's far more serious than that. Do you remember the movie Alien, when the crew of a spaceship were stuck in space with a ferocious man-eating monster that had acid for blood? This is going to be worse than Alien. I'm going to get them to eat each other.

'None of us gets out of here alive.' This really rocks them and I put my hand up in case they panic and their pacemakers overload. 'It's a figure of speech. Gentlemen, we pass this way but once, and it's our duty, our obligation, to make the world a better place for our passing. We're doing that with the Grossbank Foundation, and we need to do it with the way this mighty firm is run. We need to set the tone at the top, and if that means self-sacrifice, then so be it.'

Amazingly, they're nodding their agreement. Honour, duty, self-sacrifice all play well with this generation of Germans. Which is why none of them is cut out for investment banking.

'We need to bring down the average age of this board by twenty years, half the board should be women, and I want at least three more foreigners – don't care if they come from Timbuktu, but I want them.'

Stunned silence, then one of the fossils has a brainwave.

'But... we are the continuity of this organisation, its collective memory. That is part of the function of the board.'

It's true. These guys provide decades worth of continuity. In fact collectively they provide centuries worth. But I'm not going to argue the toss with them.

'Gentlemen, if I don't get the changes I want, the fair,

reasonable changes that will align the composition of the board with the people and interests it represents, and the modern society – the twenty-first century society – in which it operates, I will have to resign. This will be my first and last board meeting, and I will feel obliged to share with the world my reasons why. I was appointed to lead the board forward in the twenty-first century, not backwards in the nineteenth. Change is always challenging, but we must not be afraid. I've said enough, now I'm going to leave you to reflect on what I've said. I'll be in my office.'

There's an eruption of angry, puzzled, anxious voices as I leave the board room. You might think they'd be outraged by my impertinence, that they'd be vying for the opportunity to vote me off the board and fire me, but if you think that you don't know the average major corporate board. Rather than uniting against the common foe, these guys are going to devour each other. Decades of jealousy, rivalry, real and imagined slights will erupt in a vicious frenzy of in-fighting. Thirty years compressed into a couple of hours, unexpected, unscripted, just the raw savagery that only monumental, fossilised egos are capable of achieving.

The key is that I said they didn't all have to go, just some of them. If I went for the lot, they'd have taken me on. But just some? That's different.

As I leave the room, I have a spring in my step and a smile on my face. I reckon it'll take them at least an hour to accept the inevitable, maybe longer, which is plenty of time for me to get to know my new personal trainer who'll be keeping me in shape when I'm in

Frankfurt. Her name's Eva and she's blonde, well-built and athletic, as well as being very highly paid and extremely accommodating.

*       *       *

IN FACT it takes them nearly three hours, and Eva is in danger of wearing me out. But when I'm invited back into the board room they are the ones who look exhausted. They present me with a schedule of proposed retirements stretching out over the next twelve months. A few will go straight away and most of the remainder by year end. A couple of youngsters – which is to say late fifties, mere children by the standards of corporate Germany – will stay on for continuity and 'tribal memory' purposes. More of them could have stayed on, but I guess it got into one of those illogical and mutually destructive tit for tat debates. So much for grown men. And that's it. They've raised the white flag.

I love the taste of victory. Especially one that involves more or less total annihilation of the enemy. Within a few months I'll have the most exotic, best-looking board in German banking history. Naturally I'll appoint Two Livers and Paul Ryan to the board, but not Rory, and then I'll set about putting together the new look team, at least three quarters of them stunning women. My harem. They may not know much about banking, but boy will they be hot.

*       *       *

THE BLACK dogs of boredom are circling again. I'm back in London and I'm worried that even my usual pastimes are no longer keeping me entertained. Do you know how tedious it gets, screwing beautiful women, snorting coke and chugging cocktails relentlessly, night after night? No? You'll just have to trust me on that one.

The highlight of my day was chairing a new internal think-tank that I've set up. I did it for Mike Hanlan's librarian, whose real name is Caroline Connor. She's six foot one, single, academically gifted, but terribly lonely. Normally I'd do something about that myself, but at that height she's so much taller than me that I'd feel ridiculous. In case you didn't know, we are not all the same height in bed – going head to toe with an Amazon like that would stretch even my ability.

But I want to get her laid.

So I've convened a new internal think-tank comprising junior and mid-ranking employees from all parts of the firm, to think the unthinkable. What exactly does that mean? God knows. If it was thinkable I could do it myself. So these Bright Young Things will get together regularly, including a series of off-site weekends in different locations around the world, and see what sparks fly.

They are a highly elite group.

Apart from Caroline Connor, all of them are men, hand-picked by me. All the guys are single, very bright, highly competitive, over six foot three inches tall, and by my reckoning, based on the photographs in their personnel files, good looking. If she were shorter, I'd do the job myself, but I've always believed that a job worth doing is worth delegating to someone competent.

When she came into the meeting room, she almost

swooned. She thought she'd died and gone to heaven. Forget dating agencies. Think Grossbank.

Christ, I'm kind.

But also bored. Maybe that's why I was kind – I had time to play with. Tonight, I'm actually feeling so jaded that I haven't yet decided who to call. I've been debating whether to go for Ilyana again or Breathless Beth. Or maybe both. Why choose? Compromise, as I always say, is the enemy of achievement.

But perhaps neither – and anyway, they don't have the same initials, and they'd probably realise when I got them mixed up.

It's ten o'clock, I've been killing time in the office, and I'm feeling so lost that I'm only now on my way out. The trading floor is relatively empty, just a few dealers on the late shift sorting out trades with New York, and the cleaning staff getting the place ready for tomorrow.

As I pass one of the dealing desks, I see two cleaners sitting together at a workstation. They are young, black, probably late twenties or early thirties, full-bodied and large-breasted in a way that used to be called voluptuous. They look like a lot of the minimum wage migrant workers who somehow find their way into the City to perform menial tasks, their noses pressed against the glass while the rest of us are paid fortunes. They are wearing short, nylon one-piece uniforms and brightly coloured headscarves. One of them is crying.

I really don't care if people cry. It's not as if I haven't cried myself on occasion, especially in the early part of my career, normally around bonus time. But why do they have to cry in front of me? Why does everyone always feel the need to share their personal suffering? Keep it bottled up, for fuck's sake. I pause and look at the two of them. The one who's sobbing tries to stop, and they both stare up at me. They have beautiful brown eyes, skin that glows naturally, and perfectly pouting lips. I feel a vague stirring of unexpected interest.

'What's the problem, ladies?'

They look at each other, uncertain what to say. The one who was crying pulls a tissue from her pocket to wipe her eyes.

'Here.' I pass her my bright yellow silk handkerchief from the breast pocket of my jacket, the one that perfectly matches my tie. She stares at it as if it's gold, smoothing the material and looking up at me without actually using it to wipe her face. It probably cost more than she makes in a week.

'I don't mean to pry, but why were you crying?' As I say this, I pull round a chair and sit beside them. I smile, trying to look friendly, as an interesting thought comes to me, and I imagine the three of us in bed, our bodies covered in oil, rolling over together, naked…

'Please, boss…' Perfect – a woman who knows how to address me. 'Mary's cousins are all dead. They all died, sir.'

I look at the woman who was crying. I'm taken aback. 'You lost your cousins? I'm so sorry. What happened?'

She looks at me and her brown eyes are flashing with anger. She speaks with passion. 'They were killed, sir. Four boys and two girls. Murdered by the gangs.'

'Murdered? By the gangs? What gangs?'

'The gangs come to our villages in the south of our country and do this to us. They come with guns and knives and we are so poor, we can do nothing to defend ourselves.'

I'm stunned. For once I don't know what to say. Even in Brixton this doesn't happen. 'Where are you from?'

'We are from Alambo, in the East of Africa.'

Alambo. I vaguely recall it. There's been some heavy shit going on. The trouble is, I can't recall exactly what. Something to do with thousands of people homeless, or dying, or starving, or whatever. Like everyone else, when it comes to Africa I have compassion fatigue. I'm good at feeling sorry for myself, just not for anyone else. And besides, whenever the African Tragedy comes on the television news, I flick over to MTV or the Adult Channel.

I've generally found in investment banking, the greater my ignorance on any given subject, the safer it is to stick to the old saying, 'Less is more'.

'I understand.' They both look at me very directly, staring deep into my eyes. I'm not used to this kind of scrutiny, and in a way I kind of enjoy it. 'What are you going to do?'

This brings back the tears. Mary's friend, whose name I still don't know, puts her arm around her shoulders. 'She needs to return, sir. For the funerals. For the family.'

'Sure – you have to be there for your family and be supportive...'

'But she cannot.'

'She can't? What do you mean? It's a family funeral.'

The friend shakes her head. 'She cannot, because the money she earns here pays for her whole family – those that are left – it pays for them to live. And if she returned she might not have a job when she came back.'

Now even I'm shocked. 'Are you serious? Who do you work for? Who's your boss?'

Mary looks at me and seems to have a kind of fear in her eyes. 'We work for Mister Skelton.'

Skelton. I vaguely recall the name. He's Head of Premises, way down the food chain, somewhere in the semi-darkness with the tadpoles and the plankton.

'Please, boss – do you know Mister Skelton? Can you help?'

Can I help? Of course I can fucking help. I'm Dave Hart. I can do anything. I lean forward, close enough to smell their scent, feel their breath, and when I speak, I whisper so they have to lean close. 'You know the guys who run this place? The bosses?'

They shrug uncertainly. 'We've seen some of them.'

'Well, I'm their boss. The Boss of bosses. And there's someone I want you to meet.'

I get out my cell phone, scroll down the numbers until I get to 'S', and dial the Silver Fox.

\*      \*      \*

I LOVE it when a woman is grateful. I love it even more when two are. It's four in the afternoon, and I've just arrived for the morning meeting with Two Livers and Paul Ryan. Nothing unusual in that. The early edition of the Evening News is on the conference room table. Two Livers kicks off.

'Dave, you cannot be serious.' She has the paper open on a full page spread about Grossbank paying for two cleaners to fly to Alambo in a private jet with a team of bodyguards. They've had relatives murdered, and now they are returning with funds to rebuild their village. Apparently it's all down to me. The headline reads 'Hart of kindness'.

I try not to sound defensive. 'What's wrong with it?'

'Cleaners? In a smoker? To Alambo?'

'So?'

'But Dave – the cost...'

'You know what it's costing?'

'How much?'

I smile triumphantly. 'Nothing.'

'Nothing?'

'Nothing. The bank's paying. You didn't think I was picking up the tab myself, did you?'

They roll their eyes heavenwards.

'And besides, we'll cover it from what we'll save by not having a Head of Premises.'

'What do you mean?'

'Some guy called Skelton. Bad guy.' I draw my forefinger symbolically across my throat. 'He's toast. Had him black-bagged this morning.' They shrug indifferently. Survival Rule Number One for pond life: don't attract the attention of a predator. Especially a great white. 'Anyway, it's great PR.'

Two Livers frowns and stares out the window, leaving Paul to take up the cudgel. 'Dave, exactly what PR benefits are you talking about?'

'The PR. It shows how kind we are. Well, how kind I am. With the bank's money.' I grin, hoping they'll join in, but they don't.

'But Dave, it's Africa. No one cares. People really couldn't give a shit.'

He's right. If it was something serious, like the search for drugs to cure obesity, or male-pattern hair loss, we'd throw billions at it. But Africa? That's when some disconnected circuits in my brain spark briefly back to life.

'Oh, yes – that's the other thing.'

'What's that?'

'I've decided to save Africa.'

*       *       *

TO GIVE them due credit, it takes a couple of hours to bring Paul and Two Livers round. Africa is a basket case. In fact much of it is so bad it could give basket cases a bad name. But that's the opportunity. Everyone's written it off, yet there are hundreds of billions to be made out of vast mineral wealth, agri-business, real estate and tourism, to name but a few. The problem is that most firms that could invest in Africa consign it to the 'too difficult' tray – there are plenty of easier places in the world to make money, where you don't get shot or robbed or have the local bully-boys (I mean governments) running extortion rackets (I mean seeking participation in your business).

If only the place could be developed in a fair, transparent way, without most of the upside going to line the pockets of the ruling elite or being siphoned off in some sweetheart deal by bad foreign governments, rogue businessmen or Evil Empire multi-nationals, all the good guys could get involved – like our corporate clients – and think how much a firm like Grossbank could earn out of that.

That's where my plan comes in. If you really want to change something, you need to start at the top, with the guys in charge. In Africa the ruling elite, like ruling elites everywhere, like to squirrel their money away. That's where private bankers come in. Private bankers look after the money of the rich and the super-rich, politicians, businessmen, the famous and the infamous, offering discreet, private, confidential service away from the prying eyes of the great unwashed who might otherwise think they should get a slice, and certainly a long way from the regulators and the little people who make their living making sure other people pay their taxes.

If the investment banker is the social and intellectual superior of the commercial banker, the private banker is a breed apart: socially smooth and charming, well connected, mostly from old-established families, private bankers privately ooze venality and cunning. These guys have such a total lack of ethics that they make investment bankers and hedge fund managers look like paragons of moral virtue. Naturally, Grossbank has one of the biggest private banking operations in the world.

The US military used to say of 'hearts and minds' campaigns intended to win the support of indigenous peoples, forget the hearts and minds – just grab them by the balls. Grab a man's balls and pull them wherever it is you want him to go, and he will follow, because he will always want to go everywhere his balls go. Well, I can't squeeze these guys by the balls. I don't have the power to do that. But I have something even more effective. I'm going to squeeze them by the wallet. And when they smile and say 'Yes, Dave', the Grossbank legions will pile into Africa. We're going to finance mining projects, oil and gas, ranching, real estate, hotels, you name it, and we're going to do it in the places that have been written off. With their support, with them actually holding the door open for us.

We'll make billions, and it definitely won't be boring.

Two hours after I start, even I'm amazed by my sheer audacity and brilliance. Two Livers isn't so sure it will work, and we agree to our usual bet. If I win, I get a blow job. If she wins, she gets to give me a blow job. It's the sort of bet you only get to place if you're the Boss of bosses.

*       *       *

I'M BACK in Frankfurt, in my office on the fifty-fourth floor of the Grossbank Tower, staring at the elephant in formaldehyde, which seems to be staring back at me, possibly a little resentfully, which given our relative situations in life is understandable.

Whenever I visit the Fatherland, the Meat Factory get to carry real guns. It's something to do with German firearms laws, and the fact that in the past other large German banks have had their top people murdered by whackos. So today I'm sitting at my desk playing with a Walther PPK that normally sits in an ankle holster around Scary Andy's meaty lower leg. He doesn't like me playing with it, and has thoughtfully removed the bullets, since he seems to have some kind of aversion to his enthusiastically amateur boss playing with real weapons.

A low chiming sound comes from a discreetly concealed speaker, and I hit the intercom button and say 'Enter'. Then I turn my chair around so I'm facing away from the door and looking out over the Frankfurt skyline. Behind me I hear the thick oak doors swing open and footsteps getting closer. I wait until they have covered roughly three quarters of the distance to my desk before saying, half to myself, 'Damn, this is a good weapon. But I need to fire some live rounds. I need to shoot someone. Who the hell can I shoot?'

Right on cue, I hear a discreet cough behind me, and spin the chair around, pointing the gun at an early fifties, fit-looking, tall guy in a conservative suit with silver grey hair and a too perfect suntan. His name is Neumann – 'New Man' – after his father, who was one of countless Germans who found themselves in 1945 lining up to be circumcised, prior to shipping out to Argentina with their brand new names and brand new passports, claiming their families were wiped out by the Nazis and how all they were seeking was a new start. Gerhard Neumann is head of private banking at Grossbank, and he's meeting me today for the first time.

When he finds himself staring at the little black hole at the end of the barrel of the Walther he jumps. I pull the trigger.

'Click.'

For a moment he stops breathing and turns deathly pale. I imagine brown adrenaline running freely down his legs beneath his perfectly pressed trousers. I smile.

'Just joking.'

He lets out a huge sigh and when I indicate he should sit down, he flops into a large, low armchair, still staring at the empty revolver in my hand. I place it on the table and get up.

'Doktor Neumann, how very good to meet you at last. I've heard so much about you.'

He goes to stand up to shake my outstretched hand, but I wave him back down in his seat, lean over in my friendliest fashion and give him a big two-handed welcome to my lair. 'Have you met Fritz?'

'Fritz?'

I wave across to the elephant, which seems to be staring at us both. It has the sort of eyes that follow you around the room. Or maybe I'm just getting paranoid.

'N – nein. I mean, no.'

He seems really freaked out. I wonder if he actually thought I'd shoot him. I walk around behind his armchair, out of sight, then lean in suddenly so that my face is inches from his, and whisper so he can feel my breath on his cheek.

'Coffee?'

The effect is almost as electrifying as the gun. He jumps and stutters, 'Y – yes, please.'

'Good.' I smile, and lean in even closer. 'Me too. It's over there on the side. I take mine black.' I get up and walk back to my chair, sit down and watch as he scurries off to pour us a couple of coffees, then brings them back, cups rattling in the saucers in the most gratifying way as his nerves reveal him.

He's ready.

'Doktor Neumann, I've been having some thoughts about the next private banking conference for super high net worth individuals.' He looks perplexed. This is his area, and he isn't used to the Chairman getting involved. Especially a Chairman like me. 'I believe you call them 'Rich Weekends', unless I'm mistaken?'

He shrugs noncommittally. 'We try to provide our clients with the service they require.'

It's true. The rich are increasingly common, and not just because there are more of them. If they want fawning private bankers paying homage to them over a long weekend away, then that's what they'll get – for a price.

'I think the next one's in Monte Carlo next month, if my information is correct.' He nods guardedly. 'I have in mind something rather novel. I want to give it a theme. An African theme.'

'Africa?' Smooth as he is, he can't hide his scepticism.

'We look after a lot of African money.' I have some papers on my desk, positioned so that he can't actually see them. I can see him staring at them, wondering what they are – he doesn't recognise the format, it's not the usual management accounts or business area report, and he's probably wondering what kind of analysis I've got hold of relating to his notoriously private business.

In fact it's nothing to do with his business. My birthday's coming up and this is the itinerary for a special weekend away. I've rented a private Caribbean island and I'm flying out a couple of Grossbank jetloads of girls – the dream team from all over the world. I think of them as my 'All Stars', Fluffy and Thumper obviously, Crystal and Jade from Hong Kong, Tatiana from Saint Petersburg, Fifi La Poitrine from Nice, Long Suk from Korea, Breathless Beth, you name them, they'll be there, for a seventy-two hour shagathon, standing room only except when we're lying down. It'll be fantastic, as long as it doesn't actually kill me. Anyway, it takes a lot of organising.

I hold up my papers. 'I want to push the boundaries. To go into new territory. And I want to go even further.

Enough is never enough, believe me.' It's true. I smile warmly, always a dangerous moment. He seems to take it as a compliment and looks as if he's relaxing. 'I love your business, Doktor Neumann. And I want to take what you've built so carefully over these past decades and really do something with it.'

He's not sure how to take this. 'What did you have in mind?'

'First, a keynote speaker. President Mbongwe of Alambo. I'd like to invite him over to talk about the economic future of Africa.'

'Mbongwe? But he's…'

'Not a client?' I frown. 'How very disappointing.'

Now he's offended. 'Of course he's a client. We run most of his money – more than half a billion dollars.'

Gotcha. Half a billion of international aid money, licence fees for mineral rights that were never developed because the place is in meltdown, 'taxes' on investment and profits and breathing and going to the bathroom. In Alambo holding public office seems to get confused with helping yourself to public money. These guys are meant to be politicians, the leaders of their terrified, starving people – it's not as if they're investment bankers. If I had a sense of moral outrage, I'd be morally outraged. Luckily I don't, and anyway, half a billion will do nicely. 'Good. And just to be clear, I'm not simply talking about the speakers for this conference. I want the guests to have an African angle as well…'

Two days later, I have the speaker programme from hell, exceeded only by the guest list. There are former generals, politicians, freedom fighters and dictators here that I thought had died years ago, when instead they just retired quietly, slipped away to the south of France or Switzerland or some quiet Caribbean island, trotted along to their local Grossbank private banking office and bingo – shipped in their fortunes to live fat and happy for the rest of their lives. Truly private banking is the best of businesses, and truly my team have done a fine job in winning such a huge market share. I send a message to Neumann and the team saying how delighted I am, and that I will personally be attending the conference.

The great thing about the Germans, is that once you tell them which direction to go in, they are awesome. The reason the Brits still have to make jokes about the Germans several generations after we last fought each other, is that they nearly whipped our arses. The French, the Spanish, we could deal with, time and again throughout our history – they just never learnt. Despite being such a small nation, Britain could conquer half the world, but the Germans were damned scary. They even kicked the Romans' arses, and if they hadn't been fighting the rest of the world at the same time, they might have beaten Russia. Luckily we've moved on from those days. Now they're on my side. In fact they are my side. I love my Germans.

*       *       *

MY NEXT meeting is back in London. I'm meeting Ralph Jones, the head of project finance at Grossbank. Project financiers are to investment bankers what Indiana Jones is to Gordon Gekko. Unlike mainstream investment bankers, these guys are field types. Rather than visiting New York, Paris or Hong Kong, they go to Lilongwe, Yaounde and Lagos. And the biggest difference of all is that they actually make real things happen. Where the rest of us sit at our workstations and move numbers around on screens, these guys put together the finance that builds real things, like dams and mines and ports and power stations. They spend time in offbeat places living in the field with construction engineers, miners and oilmen. And when they get a result and pull together the money to build something, you can actually see what it is they've done.

If I wasn't such a wuss, I might have become one myself, only then I might not have made so much money, since people in investment banks who don't quite fit the mould tend to unsettle management and therefore don't get paid or promoted the way the rest of us do.

When Ralph enters my office, I don't invite him to sit down, but leave him standing in front of me. Without looking up, I throw my much-thumbed itinerary on the desk in front of me. He's terrified. He doesn't know what the papers are, and fears the worst. The print is too small for him to read it upside down from where he's standing, and now he's wondering what bunch of overpriced, under-qualified, no-hoper management consultants I've paid to review his business and produce recommendations for how it might be fucked-up in some big corporate restructuring of the sort that all rich, fat, successful corporations indulge in every few years.

'Ralph, I'm not a happy man.'

Strictly speaking, this is true. I have no idea what it is I'm seeking in life, all I know is that I want more of it.

But I'm not talking philosophy here. I'm talking intimidation. Then I play my ace card. I open a folder on my desk and extract a credit card slip. I say 'extract' because I hold it between thumb and forefinger as if I've found it lying, heavily soiled, on the floor of the gents. I release it and let it fall onto the desk. His eyes follow it and he tries to make out what it is. When I speak, I do so quietly, almost sorrowfully.

'What – is this?'

He stares at it, finally picks it up, recognises his signature and scrutinises it. It comes from a mid-ranking, anonymous restaurant near Bank Underground Station.

'It's a credit card slip.' I don't even bother replying to this. Some people are just too straightforward. 'It's a bill I submitted.' He looks vaguely guilty. 'I was entertaining clients. Three of them. Senior people from the Asian Development Bank.'

'Three of them?' My voice is deathly quiet.

He nods, trying to be confident, yet trying to assert his frugality.

'And you were representing this firm?' I raise my voice, almost shouting. 'My firm?'

'Y – yes. Look, if there's a problem, I'll pay it myself.'

'Of course there's a problem. You spent six... hundred... pounds...'

'Look, Mister Hart, I'm sorry. Next time...'

'Next time, you'll fucking do it properly!' I shout the words, leap to my feet and start pacing round the office, while he stands awkwardly in front of my desk like a schoolboy summoned to the headmaster's office. I almost feel it's a shame to do this to him. But he needs to be ready for what comes next. I like to soften my people up – shock and awe and all that – or maybe I'm just a bully. I lean in close to him, so I can clearly see his curiously twitching right eyelid. Don't ever play poker, pal.

'Ralph – if you ever again spend so little on what I'm laughingly told is a top ten target for the project finance team, you'll have a black bin-liner on your desk before dessert.'

'Y – you mean I didn't spend enough?'

'Of course you didn't fucking well spend enough. This...' I point dismissively at the six hundred pound credit card slip. '...This lunch for four was a disgrace. We're Grossbank. Grossbank thinks big. Grossbank is big. Do you understand big, Ralph, or are you happy to stay in your comfort zone, keeping the business small? Do you know what they say, Ralph? If you're going to bother to think, think big.'

He nods, unsure what to say next, this might be the end. He swallows hard, preparing for the worst.

'Which brings me to Africa.'

'Africa?' He almost squeaks the word. He's ready.

'I'm not happy with our project finance business in Africa.'

Silence. Fear. Dilated pupils. Slightly faster breathing. They might be project financiers, but they still have mortgages and school fees and mistresses and drug habits to pay for.

'But why not?'

'Why not? Why indeed not.' I realise I haven't prepared a set speech. 'Maybe you could tell me.' Now he's really puzzled. So am I. This tends to happen when I ad lib too much.

'Look, Mister Hart, if you're worried about our African exposure, we hardly do anything over there as it is, and if you want we can cut it out altogether. Risk Management have no appetite for it, and frankly I don't blame them. Just say the word.'

I flop back down into my chair, leaving him standing awkwardly in front of me. Now I remember. I shake my head, despairing. 'Ralph, we're not coming out of Africa. We're going in. Grossbank is going to commit fifty billion euros to investment projects in Africa over the next three years.'

'F – fifty billion? But, Mister Hart, there aren't fifty billion euros worth of projects in the whole continent.'

I lean forward and stare at him. Maybe I got the number wrong again. I hadn't really thought about it, but it seemed like a good number when I said it. Maybe I'm just not that good with numbers. When I speak, I do so slowly, as if talking to an infant. 'Not now, no. But there will be. Africa's changing, Ralph. A lot of places where it's not wise to do business today are going to be safe very shortly. Trust me on this.'

'R – right.' He's clearly unconvinced, swallows hard and bites his tongue. He thinks his boss is whacko. For all I know, he may be right.

'Ralph, I want you to do me a favour. I want you to pretend that all the worst places where you would never dream of doing business changed, and suddenly became business friendly. What would be your dream list of projects for the bank to finance? We all know there are great projects out there, if only we could get to them. And the margins would be so fat. Are you with me so far, Ralph?'

He nods, but definitely looks sceptical.

'And because the margins are so great, and we'll be making so much money, we'll do this business in an ethical way.'

'E – ethical?'

'That's right. With an 'e'. Look it up when you get back to your office.' He's looking at me now as if he expects me to burst out laughing, as if it's all a wind-up. 'We have to be consistent with the firm's image and reputation, Ralph. This has to look right.'

'Oh, I get it.' He grins at me and very nearly winks. 'It has to look right.'

This kind of pisses me off. Someone like this really should not piss me off. 'And the best way to look right, is to be right.'

'Be right?'

'Exactly. Anything we finance has to have a full environmental and social impact study – a real one, not the sort we usually pay for.'

'A real one?'

'Sure. There must be some consultants out there who can actually produce real ones?'

He looks nonplussed. Maybe there aren't. I press on. 'And our projects must source everything they can from the local economy, institute anti-corruption policies...'

'Anti-corruption? You mean...?'

I nod. 'That's right. No more 'Oh, Mister Deputy Minister, is that your wallet you appear to have dropped under the desk with five thousand dollars in it?' Those days are gone.'

At this he really does relax. 'We don't do that, Mister Hart. It's against the law.'

'So what do you do?'

Now he's nervous again.

'Come on, spill – unless you want one of these?' I open my desk drawer and pull out a black bin-liner and put it on the desk. He's transfixed. It's the equivalent of Long John Silver offering one of his pirate crew the Black Spot.

'W – well, we help our friends.'

'Help? What sort of help?'

'It depends on them. Sometimes they want to buy a house in London. We help them find bargains.'

'Bargains?'

'That's right. There are amazing bargains out there if you just… know how to look. And if they ever want to sell, we help them get a good price. A really good price. Or they want their children to get into good schools, and we help them do that – special scholarships, donations to the schools' endowment funds… and of course they sometimes want special healthcare, and there are waiting lists…'

I hold up my hand to stop him. 'I get the picture. But we don't pay bribes.'

He shakes his head. 'We don't pay bribes.'

'Good.' I put the bin liner back in the drawer and he relaxes again. 'So when can I have my list? We're about to witness a new scramble for Africa, and I want Grossbank leading it. And the number, to be clear, is fifty billion.' Or was it a hundred? I scratch my head – I'm sure I said fifty just now.

Pause. A long silence. He'd better say something soon, because I'm starting to get bored.

'Are you serious?'

'Nah, just kidding.'

'Just…? You are serious, aren't you?' He rubs his chin, thinking hard, and for the first time he actually looks excited. 'What you're asking is huge. An enormous task. I hardly know where to begin.'

'If you're not up to it, let me know.' I allow my eyes to wander towards the drawer where I keep my bin liners.

He nearly panics. 'No, we're up to it. It's just that it's so… huge.'

'Who are your biggest competitors in the market?'

'Prince's and Schleppenheim.'

'Raid their teams. Poach their best people. I'll sign the authorisations. Call them today. Buy them.' Now I really am bored. I glance at my watch. 'Look, I'd love to carry on talking about this all day – Africa, the wealth grab, changing the future, all of that, you know, but I've sort of got this bank to run…'

I usher him out of the office and tell Maria I'm going to see my chiropractor. I haven't had a blow-job since before breakfast. I think I might be addicted to sex.

*     *     *

I'M HAVING a weekend away. I'm taking a Grossbank corporate jet to Capri to a private villa owned by the bank and kept for senior management offsites and 'weekends of reflection' for board members.

Helping me reflect on this occasion will be Paula Hayes, wife of Sean Hayes, who now runs syndicated loans at Grossbank. Sean thinks his luck's in, which in a manner of speaking it is. Having been poached to run Grossbank's business on the kind of package he never dreamt of at this stage in his career, he's been amazed by the firm's commitment to what most banks see as a capital intensive, low return business. He's piling on market share, driving himself like he's never worked before in his life, because no matter how well he does, we always want more. Or at least I do. And it's working – he's made us number one in the league tables and this weekend, at my insistence, he's taking his team for an offsite in Bermuda which is part strategy session and part celebration.

It's a shame, because Paula hardly sees him as it is, and whenever we meet for a coffee on the King's Road, she's torn between thanking me for the break I've given them, and wishing she saw more of him.

In turn, I've come to rely on her for helping me to talk through my 'issues' – she's become my soulmate, or at least that's what I've told her, and occasionally I wonder if she actually believes it. And this weekend we'll take the mating aspect a stage further.

Paula's never been on a smoker before, and she's surprisingly excited. Her mother is looking after her daughter for the weekend and she's told Sean she's going on a girls' weekend away with some old university friends. She didn't take much persuading: 'It'll be good for us both. It's a change of scene, a chance to talk, a chance to think and unwind. We'll be pampered and frankly we deserve it. Neither of us has an easy time. And look – we'll have separate bedrooms and there's no obligation or expectation in any sense, okay? We're friends – soulmates.' Can you believe she fell for that? Of course she did. She's a woman and I'm Dave Hart.

Should I have a bad conscience? Nah. Who wants to be good? Life is too short to be good. Look at it this way – her husband got a fantastic break, he's making out like a bandit, and within a few months of arriving at Grossbank, they're already planning to buy a house in Holland Park and talking about having another child. Meanwhile Paula's life has been spiced up by having some excitement in it. She gets to fly in a smoker, drink fine champagne, eat caviar, do a few lines of coke, and get screwed by me – and yes, I bet she turns out to be a screamer. Life is good in the Hayes household. There won't be any emotional commitment, because we're about to become fuckbuddies – friends with benefits, as the Americans say – and since we're grown-ups we both know it can't go anywhere, and we'll enjoy it while it lasts. Or at least I will.

\*     \*     \*

COMMUNICATION HAS to be one of the most important aspects of investment banking. We don't always get it right.

After getting back from Capri, refreshed and rejuvenated – and yes, she is a screamer – I've headed straight off to Asia. I'm sitting on the terrace of the Shanghai Oriental, half way through a whistle stop tour of Grossbank's Asian operations, with Paul Ryan. Whenever I feel I need a change of scene, I come to Asia. The girls are more compliant, the oils they rub into you more exotic, and from time to time I even squeeze in a useful business meeting.

We're dressed in chinos and Hawaiian shirts, and Paul is wearing dark glasses at night, which I always find incredibly cool, mainly because if I do it I keep bumping into things. We're just sipping our first cocktail of the evening, when Paul mutters, half to himself, 'There are some mossies around tonight.'

'Some Aussies? Where?'

'Everywhere. I hate the fuckers.'

'Really? I had no idea.'

'Oh, come on – everyone does. You can't get away from them.'

'Well, I suppose we are in China. You'd expect a few. It's kind of their home territory.'

He gives me a curious sideways glance. 'It's not just China. You get them everywhere. And they spread diseases.'

'Really?'

'Oh, come on, Dave. Have you taken something? Anyway, if it was my choice, I'd wipe them out. Total eradication.'

I'm shocked. Normally Paul is so tolerant. Maybe it's a gay thing. The Aussies have this kind of false machismo, whereby they try to persuade the rest of us that they're just a bunch of straightforward, barbie-loving, beer-swilling, lovable rogues, when in reality I'm sure a lot of them are as full of complexes, neuroses and metaphysical anguish as the rest of us, plus I bet they're homophobic as well.

Personally I'm extremely tolerant of gay men. The more gay men there are, the less competition there is for beautiful women. Or perhaps it's just that I don't care – on reflection, I don't think I'm tolerant at all, just self-obsessed and indifferent.

Paul shifts uncomfortably in his chair. 'It's the noise they make that really gets to me. Especially when they get close.'

I find this puzzling. It's true that the Australian accent isn't necessarily the most romantic on earth – a French woman can read the weather report and seduce me – but compared to, say, a young German couple exchanging guttural utterances in the moonlight, the Aussie accent is okay. And besides, how close does Paul get to Australians?

He's rubbing the back of his neck and looks uncomfortable. 'I've had it. I'm out of here. Can't deal with them.'

I'm shocked. I look around. There are some expat types drinking in the bar, but I can't hear any Australian accents. 'What do you mean, you're out of here? Just because of some Aussies?'

'Yep. Do you want another drink or shall I get the check on my way out?'

I'm staggered. I return to my room and call Two Livers in London.

'We're closing Sydney and Melbourne.'

'Why? We've only just hired investment banking teams in both places. Good people.'

'I don't care. Executive decision. Trust me on this one. And get me the personnel files of any Australians working in the London office. On my desk when I get back.'

I owe Paul this one. He was there when we first got Grossbank started in the investment banking business, and if he can't stand these guys, then neither can I. Total eradication.

\*       \*       \*

MONACO HAS to be one of the least pleasant places on earth, which in a way is appropriate, because it attracts some of the least pleasant people on the planet. I'm here, for starters. And with me are the cream of Grossbank's worldwide private banking team. Amidst the concrete and glass and the tasteless glitz and the hookers and the super-yachts, I feel quite at home. The girls here are amazing, and you can rent them by the yard, all shapes and sizes, all tastes catered for. This is my kind of place. No one, no matter how jaded his appetite, need ever be bored in Monte Carlo. It makes Sodom and Gomorrah look like the Pleasure Beach at Blackpool.

The Grossbank building is one of the largest and most in-your-face with expensive art, air conditioning so cold you feel you'll go down with pneumonia, and deep shag carpets that you could almost swim through. It's full of private banking types, and they all treat me like God, which I rather enjoy. They've cleared out the top floor with its marvellous harbour views, for my personal use, and seem put out when I decline the services of two of the most glamorous personal assistants on the Grossbank payroll. Unusually for me, I've work to do.

It's Rich Weekend and I've flown in with Two Livers and the Meat Factory. The Silver Fox is already here with a whole team of his people. I'm getting ready to present to a hand-picked gathering of fifty or so super high net worth clients, which is to say individuals who have stolen more money than Al Capone could dream of and better yet have got away with it. At least until now.

'Ladies and gentlemen, for those of you who don't yet know me, I'm Dave Hart, Chairman of Grossbank.

Please allow me to welcome you to Grossbank's thirty-fifth annual investment conference for private banking clients. In a moment our head of private banking, Gerhard Neumann, will explain the detailed programme that we've got lined up for you.' Pause for big smile. 'We have some treats in store. John Highway, of Downtown Capital, will be speaking about 'When the music stops: alternative investments and the future of the hedge fund industry'. That should be a short talk.' Pause for polite laughter. 'And Ron Monk, of Toddlers Group, has a great presentation on shareholder activism entitled 'Terror in the boardroom – creating mayhem in a good cause'. As you know, Toddlers Group give away a large chunk of their profits to charity, which gives them a kind of special licence to terrorise the boards of large corporations who need to raise their game. That presentation will be illustrated and we advise vegetarians and the squeamish not to attend.' That brings a few more polite titters. These guys are not squeamish. 'But the keynote speaker, who will be joining us this afternoon, is President Mbongwe of Alambo. He will be speaking to us this evening about the economic future of Africa, and we look forward to that very much. As you meet the other guests here this weekend, you will notice a particular African theme among them. We have assembled an interesting cross-section of current and former political leaders, businessmen and others with major interests in the region, and we hope you will have an interesting and useful time networking as well as listening to our speakers. And there will, of course, be the usual entertainment that is customary on these occasions.' That gets a few knowing smiles. It's not as if we've booked the Three Tenors. The entertainment for these guys (and the few women who are present) will take place in the privacy of their hotel suites, organised with all the attention to detail and discretion that you would expect of a top private banking organisation.

With the intros done, I go up to the top floor office and work on the President's speech with Two Livers and the Silver Fox. Neumann joins us and he's sweating despite the air conditioning. 'Mister Hart, are you sure you don't want to re-consider? Are you being perhaps a little rash? We have our principles to think of, our legal obligations, our business ethics…'

'Stop.' I love the Germans. All it takes is one word and he shuts up. That's discipline for you. 'We've been through this already. Don't play the morality card with me. Do you recall why we're doing this?'

He does. 'The profit…'

'Wrong.'

'Wrong? But I thought you said…'

'I did. But it's not just about profit.' Two Livers is giving me one of her 'will you ever stop bullshitting' looks, but grinning at the same time. 'We're doing this for the poor people.'

'The poor people? What do you mean?'

'The poor people. You must have seen them.' For a moment he looks uncertain. 'The problem with Africa is the poor people. It's the same with Britain. The rich aren't the problem. Back home in London you won't find rich people hanging around in dark alleyways at night waiting to rob old ladies. Why would they? And Africa is even worse. In whole chunks of Africa there isn't even anyone worth robbing. So what we have to do is eliminate all the poor people. They're an embarrassment.'

Two Livers sighs and stares out at the boats. The Silver Fox is giving me a funny look. Neumann seems perplexed.

'Eliminate them?'

'That's right. Watch my lips – no… poor… people.'

'But how?'

'By making them rich. Well, not exactly rich. We don't want them turning into us. But at least middle class. We need to turn them into consumers, we need them to worry about whether they have the latest iPod or sufficient bandwidth on their home broadband or the correct features on their mobile phone or whether their new car has the right satnav. The important things in life, at least if you're middle class. It's the twenty-first century and they should have all the same neuroses and complexes and hang-ups as the rest of us. They shouldn't have to worry about finding food, or whether someone's going to burn their village down. Should they?'

He shrugs. 'Well, no, of course not, but can't we just give some money to the international agencies, and leave our governments to…?'

'Hell, no! We've been doing that for years. It hasn't worked. Not only has it not worked, but it's comprehensively failed. So now it's capitalism's turn. Greed is good, and money can fix anything. When you look back on your career, and your grandchildren ask you what you did, you'll tell them about this. You were there with Dave Hart and you helped to make it happen.'

He seems almost wistful, but then his mobile rings and

he turns pale. 'The President's plane has landed – he's on his way from the airport.'

I glance at my watch. There's a private room at the back of the office, next to the executive bathroom. I probably have twenty minutes. I flick the intercom and call through to the branch manager.

'Could you send through my personal assistants?'

\*　　\*　　\*

PRESIDENT MBONGWE is utterly charming. He's mid-fifties, portly, with a beaming wide smile and a bone-crunching handshake. He's wearing a dark blue, pin-stripe suit that looks like it came from Savile Row, a silk tie and matching handkerchief and handmade leather shoes. He has a chunky gold Rolex on his wrist, and arrives in my office wearing sunglasses, which he obligingly removes when he sits down, so that I can stare into his cold, hard, bloodshot eyes.

I'm not wearing sunglasses, which means that he is free to stare back into my warm, friendly, bloodshot eyes.

President Mbongwe loves his people. If the press reports are true he loves them boiled, roasted and grilled. He has a big laugh, the way people do when they've had a million or so of their fellow countrymen killed, while a couple million more – no one really knows – starved to death. Luckily for him the holocaust in Alambo clashed with Talent YooKay, or maybe it was Xtreme Idol, and so nobody noticed.

He has his right hand man with him, his personal financial adviser, who is altogether different. Sam Walsh is American, early forties but prematurely greying in an elegant, patrician way, from a well-to-do family. Slick, well turned out, he used to work for Hardman Stoney before striking it rich advising President Mbongwe. As villains go, he is altogether different from his boss. Sam went to Harvard Business School, and villains don't come any more civilised than that. The moment he walks in I know I'm not going to like him.

We sit down at the conference table with Two Livers, while my frazzled-looking personal assistants pour coffee, ignoring the lascivious glances of the President. Walsh doesn't seem to notice them, and I wonder if he's gay, but then I see him looking at Two Livers and now I really can't stand the motherfucker.

Neumann joins us and sits uncomfortably at the end of the table, as if seeking to distance himself from what is about to happen.

'Mister President, you've been a client of Grossbank for nearly ten years.'

He smiles. 'That's right, Mister Hart. Ten happy, prosperous years. God has smiled upon me, and my fortunes have increased remarkably.'

I'm looking at some sheets of numbers on the table in front of me, and for once they are genuine. 'Yes, it is remarkable, isn't it? And while I'm pleased to see that the Grossbank investment management team have made wise decisions on your behalf, you have also received substantial inflows of funds from elsewhere.'

He beams across at me. 'Indeed, from many places. Truly I have been blessed, Mister Hart.'

'Until now, Mister President.' He starts as I say this, and beside him Walsh fixes me with a laser beam stare.

'I have here your latest portfolio performance figures from the investment management team. Relating to last month.' I look across at Walsh. 'I don't believe you've seen these numbers yet, Mister Walsh?'

Walsh looks flustered and glances at his boss. 'We normally get those numbers in a few days' time, just around the start of the following month. Is there something unusual about the latest numbers?'

I nod and slide a bar chart across the table. It shows the President's portfolio growing steadily month by month as Grossbank's finest brains put his money to work in the cleverest ways they could to make him ever richer. At the end of the previous month, he had five hundred and fifty million dollars with us.

This month he had zero.

Walsh laughs. 'Is this some kind of joke?' He turns to his boss, who is allowing his face to relax into a malevolent stare. 'This guy's crazy. You don't lose half a billion in a single month.' He looks at the others, as if for support or validation, but Two Livers stares icily back while Neumann wipes his brow with his handkerchief.

'I'm afraid your boss just did.' I say the words so quietly that both Walsh and Mbongwe have to strain to hear.

Walsh is about to say something when the President's booming voice cuts him off. 'I want my money!' His fist slams down on the table, Neumann looks as if he's about to wet himself, and Two Livers and I stare implacably back.

'Mister President, you don't seem to be listening.' This is Two Livers, her voice sexy, husky, measured. 'What Mister Hart just told you is that you don't have that money any more. It's gone – all of it. Sometimes the value of investments goes up, sometimes it goes down. In your case it went all the way down. Let's just say it was a bad month.'

Walsh leaps to his feet. 'Listen, you blonde bitch – you don't know who you're dealing with. If you think you can rip us off, you better think again.' He draws his finger menacingly across his throat and then points at her aggressively. 'We don't fire people, we shoot them!'

I look at him quizzically. 'Did you say bitch?'

He looks at me as if I'm nuts. Underneath the table, I press a buzzer to the outer office and the doors swing open to allow the Meat Factory to march in, lining up behind Mbongwe and Walsh. They do nothing, say nothing, just stand there. It's enough. Walsh sits back down. The President's eyes no longer seem hard and menacing, but piggy and scared, darting to and fro, wondering what's going to happen next.

I lean forward. 'Mister Walsh, did you say bitch?'

'So what if I did? Where's our half billion?'

I nod to Scary Andy, who's briefed on what to do next. He strides over to the huge floor to ceiling windows and slides one of them open, allowing the warm breeze from the harbour far below to rustle the papers on the desk.

I stare hard at Walsh. 'Mister Walsh, can you fly?'

Walsh is – finally – lost for words. He looks at the open window, hears the faint sound of traffic in the street far below, looks at Andy and the rest of the Meat Factory, and finally looks at his boss, who turns away, as if it doesn't concern him. 'I – I didn't mean it...'

'But are you sorry?'

He really can't believe this is happening to him. We

should be fawning over them, doing the usual private banking sycophant on steroids act.

'Y – yes...'

'Well, say so then.'

'I... I'm sorry. I didn't mean it. I apologise.'

I turn to Two Livers. 'Miss MacKay, are you prepared to accept Mister Walsh's apology?'

She sighs, seems uncertain, as if making a difficult decision, looks at the open window, at the now blubbering Walsh, and finally nods her head. 'Okay.'

Andy closes the window, Walsh slumps in his seat, and I place another piece of paper on the table.

'Mister President, Grossbank would like to help you. Because we're in the happiness business. And we want to make you happy again. In fact we want to make you happier than you've ever been before.' I smile, just so he can get some idea of quite how happy we'd like him to be. His scared, piggy eyes dart down to the proposal I'm sliding across the table to him. 'We have what we call our Fast Asset Recovery Team. I'd like you to meet them.' I press the buzzer again and this time Ralph Jones, Grubmann and Kuntz come in – the Good, the Bad and the Ugly. The Mountain Troll pulls out a chair next to Mbongwe and lowers his enormous bulk onto it, smiling reassuringly and causing the President to lean away towards Walsh on his other side. Walsh is also leaning inwards, away from Werner Grubmann, who has sat beside him and unleashed a wave of toxic halitosis. Only Ralph Jones remains standing, weighed down with an armful of files – a bauxite project in Northern Alambo, oil projects in the south, a hydro dam, a new airport, a micro-finance fund for the small farmers in the east of the country. Altogether he has more than thirty files. 'Mister President, these are our best people. We want to place you in their hands.' Mbongwe still looks nervous. I'm not sure he wants to be in the Troll's meaty hands. 'We want to get them to work on your situation. We believe that an aggressive investment strategy can recoup all of your funds and make you far wealthier than before in a very short space of time. Alambo will have to change, naturally, but it can look forward to a golden age, and you will prosper with your fellow countrymen, as a truly enlightened leader should. However, I have to say this particular programme is performance-related, and it's not for everyone. We're offering this only to select clients who are working with us on our plan for Africa. What do you think, Mister President – are you with us?'

\*       \*       \*

COMPARED TO Mbongwe, the other meetings are a breeze. In fact after a while, we start to have a laugh. We're sitting facing Michel De Winter, a Belgian billionaire who made his money out of conflict diamonds in West Africa, and has arrest warrants outstanding in much of the civilised world, which is why he only comes to places like Monaco. When he hears how his portfolio did last month, he has a serious sense of humour failure.

Two Livers is sitting beside me, punching numbers into a laptop. As she types, the words come up on a screen at the end of the conference room.

De Winter snarls at us, 'You bastards. You're just common thieves.'

Dead pan, I turn to Two Livers. 'Miss MacKay, Mister De Winter just gave twenty million dollars to the Green Africa Fund.'

She types in the numbers, presses Enter, and on the screen the words 'Transaction Accepted' flash up.

'Real time banking, Mister De Winter. Now, shall we talk?'

'You scum. You'll pay for this.' He's literally spitting his anger across the table.

'Mister De Winter, it pains me to see you like this. I like you. Well, maybe not... Miss MacKay, that's another twenty mill, this time for the campaigning charity LaTiA. That's Liberty and Transparency in Africa, Mister De Winter.'

Eventually he gives in. They all do when they feel that deadly tightening around their wallets.

We meet General Mick van Smit, a South African-born mercenary leader – sorry, international security adviser – who runs the armed forces of the Democratic Republic of Lubumbashi. Lubumbashi, like any country that has the word Democratic in its name, is a dictatorship. When Smit has had his initial shock and made the usual threats, Two Livers produces tarot cards and starts laying them out on the table.

'General, I can see great good fortune ahead of you. You are going to become wise and benevolent and be greatly adored by the common people. To begin with, you are going to enforce law and order in the eastern jungles, and allow the people to return to their homes...'

'The hell I will,' he roars back.

I chime in at this point. 'Thank you, General. That's twenty million dollars to the African Reconstruction Fund.'

'What are you talking about?'

'It's a donation. You just made a donation. Very generous.'

Two Livers continues. 'And then I see you instructing the warlords to leave the poor villages of the western plains alone, and return to their own lands.'

'Bullshit.'

'Congratulations, General, that's another twenty mill, this time for Action Africa's human rights campaign.'

Two Livers continues. 'And you will advise the President to allow the aid agencies to return.'

This time he pauses, his eyes darting between Two Livers and me. He rubs his chin. 'That might be possible...'

'Looks like you just got some back!' I smile and offer him my hand across the table in a high five, but he sits back, disbelieving.

By this time even Neumann is smiling and starting to loosen up and have a little fun. He had no idea we could do things like this – breaking the law, stealing clients' money, threatening to throw them out the window and so on. It isn't what private bankers usually do, but we're Grossbank, and Grossbank rocks.

Eventually they all crumble. And when they truly cannot believe their misfortune, when their world – or at least their fortune – has fallen apart, we offer them hope. Because we're really nice guys and Grossbank is in the happiness business.

\*     \*     \*

JUST IN case you think I'm soft, and might have overlooked something, there's one more wrinkle. It's one thing to get these guys to agree things sitting in the Grossbank building in Monaco, potentially quite another to enforce it once they leave. That's where my real heavies come in. My legal heavies.

Lawless, Hood and Partners are one of Wall Street's most powerful law firms. They're not in the phone book, and they don't have a website. They have only ten clients, all of whom pay well over ten million dollars a year just by way of a retainer to ensure they get access to the firm when they need it. Their clients include several of America's richest billionaires, a sprinkling of large corporates – let's just say a major software company, a leading defence contractor and one or two other friendly household names – and guess who else...

Sam Walsh looks pretty cocky when he goes off to a separate meeting room with Ralph Jones. He probably thinks he can outsmart Ralph when it comes to contract law, disclosure and legal enforceability. But he gasps as the meeting room door opens and six US attorneys walk in. These guys are like Robocop with a law degree. To begin with, they all look alike: dark suits, dark ties, white shirts, dark glasses, identical brown leather briefcases for their laptops and 'pilot bags' full of documents, broadly similar 'Ken Doll' good looks and short haircuts. The team leader is probably early fifties, but very trim, and the only real distinguishing feature between him and the rest of the team is his slightly greying hair. Until he holds out his hand to Sam Walsh.

'Mark Hood. Senior partner, Lawless, Hood.'

Walsh goes pale and swallows hard. These guys are the legal equivalent of the Meat Factory. They sit down, open their briefcases, fire up their laptops, and start work. Their operating style is legendary. They go all the way through to the end of the assignment, all night long if necessary, without removing their jackets or loosening their ties, without stopping for coffee or sending out for sandwiches, without even a comfort break. The pace is relentless, and unforgiving. They're like Olympic athletes, only fitter and stronger. Or maybe giant squid, with their tentacles around you. Either way, when you're in their grip, you might as well give up.

Faced with my legal storm troopers, and knowing that resistance is futile, Walsh gives up, the same as all the rest.

*     *     *

PRESIDENT MBONGWE is about to give his speech. We've booked the whole of Chez Albert, a Michelin three-star restaurant close to the Casino. Our guests seem more subdued than usual, but I suppose that's understandable under the circumstances. Unusually for a private banking event, we've allowed a very select group of journalists into the back of the restaurant to hear the speech. Before he goes up to the podium, Mbongwe and Walsh corner me and Ralph Jones. Walsh looks exhausted, half the man he was when he arrived. The team from Lawless, Hood have worked him over thoroughly, the agreements are watertight, and he has no place to hide. The President on the other hand is looking anxious, and when he's scared he gets mean.

'Mister Hart, I want you to know, I have a long memory and I bear grudges.'

I believe him. Apparently he keeps the heads of people he has grudges against in the freezer in his palace in Alambo. Investment bankers can be a pretty mean lot, but we don't go that far.

'I understand, Mister President, but you have to see this from my perspective. I would never really have taken all that money from your account.'

'You wouldn't?' He looks surprised.

'Well, maybe... Let's just say I needed to get your attention, to persuade you to share in the vision that Ralph and the team laid out.' I turn to Ralph Jones. 'Did you go through the details of the royalty schemes with Mister Walsh?' They both nod and I turn back to Mbongwe. 'Your royalties will make you feel like royalty, Mister President. In a few years you'll be able to retire richer than you ever imagined.'

'I could imagine a lot, Mister Hart.'

'Me too.'

'So how much will I have? Billions?'

'Billions. More than you could ever spend.'

He looks to Walsh for confirmation. Walsh has been going through Ralph's folders of projects that will transform the country, jet propelling its economic development, all financed by guess who, and carried out by guess whose corporate clients. 'But I could spend a lot.'

'Me too. I can relate to that.' He smiles, I smile and we shake hands. We're going to get along fine, though when the money does come through, I think he might spread it around a few other banks...

When Mbongwe steps up to the podium, a curious hush descends around the room. This man is known as a serious bad guy. What on earth can he ever say about the future economic development of Africa, given what he's done to his own country?

'Ladies and gentlemen, it's a pleasure and a privilege to be here tonight, amongst such distinguished company.' They shift uncomfortably. They know, and he knows, and they know that he knows, that a more insalubrious gathering of villains, thugs and gangsters would be hard to find anywhere on the planet, even in Monaco.

'Tonight, I want to draw a line under the past. Under all of our pasts. I want to join with Dave Hart, our host, and the team from Grossbank, in launching their New Start for Africa Campaign.' New Start was the Silver Fox's idea. I thought of BankAid, but that was dismissed as too derivative – it's been done before. Neumann wanted Projekt Afrika – Unterstützung und Wiederaufbau – which is apparently quite snappy if you're German.

The President continues. 'I come from a troubled land. A land that has struggled with poverty in the harshest of climates. And if I look inside my own heart, I cannot say that I have always done all that was best for my country.' There's a stirring of surprise among the journos at the back of the restaurant. 'I could have done – should have done – much more. And so tonight I want to be the first African leader to support Grossbank's new initiative, its New Start for Africa campaign. Many western banks and financial institutions shy away from Africa. They fear the Dark Continent. But this man – ' Mbongwe turns and points at me, sitting at the nearest table in front of the podium. 'This man knows no fear, except perhaps the fear of failure to do what is right.' When I first heard it, I loved this last bit: the Silver Fox at his eloquent best. 'In a moment, Dave Hart will be announcing the details of the fifty billion euro commitment that Grossbank will be making to Africa, starting with its investment programme in my own country. Ladies and gentlemen, let us toast a new age.'

The applause is a little muted, though Mbongwe is genuinely happy. I wonder if he really did want to be a bad guy. As psychopathic cannibals go, he really isn't so bad. When we offered him a way out, a chance to rehabilitate himself – and get hugely rich in the process – he seized it. Under our agreement, he has five more years. Five years to build the democratic institutions for an eventual handover of power when he retires to a private island in the Caribbean, his fortune safe and intact, his place in the history books secure.

Following his speech, I do a brief outline of New Start, emphasising the fundamentally commercial nature of our commitment – I don't want to cause another run on the share price – and then members of the audience leap to their feet and 'spontaneously' make pledges in front of the journos. General Mick van Smit has been in touch with his President, and they want to work with us to draw up a Grossbank New Start plan for Lubumbashi. He's ordering in the army to clear out the warlords and secure the necessary stability for our investment to work. Michel de Winter wants to do something similar for the West African diamond fields. And so it goes on. It's amazing how generous bad people can be. If you thought charity auctions in the City could be surprising, you should have been at Rich Weekend. Giving as a competitive sport. And all in a good cause – on Monday morning, Grossbank's stock goes up five per cent.

\* \* \*

I'M BACK in London, and Maria is away. Of all things, she's doing jury service. We got her out of it twice already, claiming urgent work commitments, but now they are saying she has no more jokers to play. Quite why we need juries is beyond me. If the police have taken all the trouble to charge someone, they must be guilty. Anyway, she's not around, so now I'm having to cope with a yah-yah blonde air-head with a degree in Sleep Studies from the University of Cornwall at Rock, who knows nothing and can't organise her way out of a paper bag, but at least wears short skirts and has great tits.

This morning I'm calling my doctor's surgery, doing it myself because I have no one competent to delegate it to. Have you noticed how doctors' receptionists grill you on your condition, assessing you for suitability to see their boss, acting as gatekeeper as if they were actually capable of making medical assessments over the telephone? It really pisses me off.

'What's your condition, Mister Hart?' The voice is Sloaney, expensively educated but thoroughly dim. She manages to give the impression that I'm incredibly privileged that she's actually dealing with me and can I please hurry up because she has other far more important things to do.

'I'm discharging pus from the end of my penis.'

'Oh, really?' She sounds gratifyingly shocked and revolted.

'Yes, and the scabs and lesions around the base are also leaking, although I stopped picking them weeks ago.'

'Oh...' She sounds like she's going to throw up.

'There's a lot of blood in the pus, and blood and yellowish-green pus in my urine when I pee.'

Silence. At the other end I can picture her retching, holding the handset from her ear in case I infect her telephonically. 'W – would tomorrow at nine o'clock be satisfactory?'

'Yes, it would. Thank you.'

I hang up. Actually, I've been reviewing my jabs ahead of going to Singapore for the IMF conference. I've decided I'm due for an anti-tetanus shot, but why should she know that?

*       *       *

IT'S SATURDAY and I'm going to Glyndebourne with Two Livers as the guest of my new best friend, Vlad the Impaler from First Siberian Bank. Tom is going to drive us down mid-afternoon, so we start at her flat in Mayfair with champagne breakfast in bed.

The great thing about having sex – I mean breakfast – with Two Livers is that she always makes me laugh. I arrive hungover and feeling sorry for myself, which she was expecting. She welcomes me dressed only in a long silk nightgown that is tied sufficiently tightly by a cord around the waist that it reveals her breasts perfectly through the material.

I follow her into the kitchen, where she's prepared a

potent cocktail mixture – she calls it her 'Corpse Reviver' – which she pours into a cocktail shaker full of crushed ice. She then turns her back to me and says, 'Dave, do me a favour – hold my tits, will you?'

While I stand behind her keeping her 34DD's under control, she shakes the mixture like a woman possessed. And of course, once we start laughing, one thing leads to another... and another... and another. Naturally I'm still Viagra-ed up from the night before. Afterwards, when we've showered – more delay – and got dressed – more delay half-way through, when I see the lingerie she's wearing – she does one of the sexiest things a woman can do for a man. She ties my bow tie – from behind.

Glyndebourne being the formal, ritualistic place it is, with more or less compulsory black tie for the men and evening dress for the ladies – though what that means these days is anyone's guess – we're going down there in all our finery. Two Livers is wearing a plain black Armani dress that clings to her perfect form, and is set off brilliantly by a diamond necklace and earrings that must have cost well into six figures. She stands behind me as I look at myself in her full-length bedroom mirror. I'm fully dressed save for the bow tie hanging round my neck. She rests her head on my shoulder, threads her hands through my arms and gently runs her fingernails across my chest through my shirt. It's electrifying. She's wearing wicked bright red nail varnish and I sigh pathetically and very nearly spin around and say forget the opera, but then she carefully and competently takes the ends of my tie and ties a perfect bow, tweaking it tight and turning it just slightly to one side so that no one will believe such a perfect bow might be a pre-tied elasticated version of what a gentleman should wear.

She doesn't say a word, she's slow, sexy and respectful, almost submissive, and it's nearly as good as sex. Our eyes meet in the mirror. Later. Again. For sure. Damn, she's good.

\*     \*     \*

THE JOURNEY down is miserable. The roads are crowded with poor people driving themselves in crappy cars, or worse still people who think they've made it, driving themselves badly in expensive, high-powered cars that they should never really be let loose in – Beemers, Astons, Mercs, all names I used to aspire to in the old days.

My convoy stays together, however aggressive they have to be towards other road users, because the team in the Range Rovers won't allow us to be separated. When we're close to Glyndebourne, we cut up a guy in a DB9 wearing a dinner suit and driving a glamorous, dark-haired woman with a very low cut dress, whom I recall as a Brazilian hooker from one of the top agencies – definitely not a cheap date.

He blasts his horn but we ignore him and drive on.

When we get to the car park, he's following us, and pulls up next to one of the Range-Rovers. They have blacked-out glass, otherwise he might not have been so rash. He probably thinks he'll find a fat retired banker and his fatter wife inside. He might even have it in mind to cause a scene and intimidate them. Anyway, he throws open his car door and leaps out, a ginger-haired guy in his late twenties, all high testosterone and executive aggression, and I wonder if one day his dick will grow to normal size and he'll buy a proper car and start to act like a grown-up. Looking at him, I remember him as a hedge fund manager, a finance rock star who talks the talk and just possibly might believe he can walk the walk.

At least until the doors of the Range-Rover open – all four doors at once – and he finds himself facing four men who might have been picked straight out of the front row of the England rugby team, if only the England rugby team weren't such wusses. They ignore him, and the words die on his lips. But then he catches sight of Two Livers and me getting out of the Merc.

'Hey, you – Dave Hart.'

He must have seen my picture somewhere. I don't like talking to strangers, at least not unless they are female and very exotic. I think of myself as a quiet, shy, retiring sort of guy. So I ignore him too.

'Oi, didn't you hear me?'

He comes striding round the front of the Range-Rover, towards the Merc, ignoring the fact that all four heavies are moving in on him, while on the other side of the Merc four more from the second Range-Rover have clocked him too. Tom has spotted him and gets out of the Merc, positioning himself between Mister Angry and us.

He's wearing a bright red bow tie that marks him out as one of a self-styled elite drinking club called the Flaming Fiascos. These guys think they are really hot, and have a reputation for trashing expensive restaurants and spoiling other people's evenings, all of which they put right by waving their magic cheque books around. I condemn such vulgar, over-the-top behaviour unreservedly, particularly since they never invited me to join. Meanwhile the street-smart Brazilian spots the danger her man is in and she's tottering after him as fast as her high heels will allow, calling out to him to 'cool it'.

'I know who you are, you wanker.'

I turn and smile, and pat Tom on the shoulder. 'Did you hear that? He called you a wanker.'

Two Livers agrees. 'I did. I definitely heard him call you a wanker, Tom.'

Tom is blocking his way, and all around him the Meat Factory are forming up.

'Not you – him.' The guy is pointing at me. His voice has risen and he's looking a little less angry now. 'He's a wanker.' He sees Tom's jaw clench, and takes a step backwards, eyes widening as he realises he's about to discover the difference between executive aggression in the dealing room and the real thing.

Tom pats him on the shoulder. 'I think it's your birthday…'

There are those who say that standards of behaviour have dropped at Glyndebourne in recent years, probably because of all those boisterous City types with more money than sense. But it really is too much for some of the old traditionalists when what is obviously a rugby club outing gets carried away.

I can almost hear them tutting as a group of prop forwards carry one of their smaller team mates, probably the scrum half, struggling and protesting, shoulder high, while they laugh and sing 'Happy Birthday', and throw him in the lake.

Boys will be boys.

\*　　　\*　　　\*

TWO LIVERS and I go through to the bar where Vlad the Impaler is waiting for us with his girlfriend of the moment, a stunning Oriental type with long dark hair and a classic hour glass figure, who apparently comes from one of the Central Asian republics. Vlad is married, but Mrs Kommisarov prefers to stay at home.

He has another guest, an Icelander called Ras Rasmussen, early thirties, very tall with long fair hair tied in a pony-tail and an athletic physique. This man could be an Australian lifeguard, if he wasn't the billionaire owner of SmegBank, a new and very aggressive entrant to the Square Mile that has come from nowhere and now seems to be buying up great British brand name companies at the rate of about one a month. He's very cool, very handsome, and as soon as he sees Two Livers his mouth drops open, his tongue hangs out, and he ignores his cute blonde Icelandic wife.

She looks about six months pregnant – their second child – and my guess is that he's reached the coyote stage of pregnancy, so starved of sex that he's howling for it. To make matters worse, instead of joining us all in a glass of champagne, he's clutching a beer bottle in his hand – a Zero, the new low-calorie, alcohol-free beer for fags. Clearly, we're not going to get on.

It gets worse. It turns out Ras is a toy collector. Not children's toys, but adult ones. He has six homes, in all the usual places, a small fleet of classic cars, a super-yacht that spends the winter in the Caribbean and the summer in the Med, and a private jet.

'Just the one?'

He looks irritated by my question. At Grossbank, Two Livers and I have the run of the entire air force, but it's not the same – we don't have to worry about servicing the planes or paying the crew, because everything's free.

I used to be an aspiring toy collector myself, running on the treadmill to assemble the most impressive collection I could before I died – he who dies with the most toys wins – but now it just seems empty. Partly it's because it's an unwinnable contest – there's always a Russian oligarch or Indian steel magnate with more than you – and partly it's because it gives me a sense of accumulating baggage. I'd rather rent someone else's headache. But what do I do instead? All I seem to do is focus on momentary pleasures and let the money pile up in my bank account. What's it all for? I start to feel a blackie coming on, so I hit the champagne even harder.

Over a couple of magnums of champagne we cover all the usual tedium that we have to talk about when someone brings their wife to what would otherwise be an enjoyable and lively event. Ras's wife has only lived in London for a couple of months, and wants to ask all kinds of dumb questions.

'Our son is three years old. His name is Sven.' I groan. Any second now she'll open her handbag and get out the photos. 'Do you have children, Mister Hart?'

'Call me Dave. Only one that I know of.'

'One child?' She smiles sweetly at her husband, who is

staring at the outline of Two Livers' nipples through her dress. 'The same as us.' She rubs her tummy and does look kind of cute – her eyes are shining and she has that special look that pregnant women sometimes get. 'But soon we will have two.' Oh really, I hadn't noticed. She looks as if she thinks I'm going to ask if she knows the sex of her second child, but instead I pour myself another glass of champagne, so she carries on relentlessly. 'Do you have a girl or a boy?'

'Girl… I think. Yeah, a girl. Called Samantha, four years old, lives with her mother, Wendy. We're divorced.' I know I'm being a wanker, but I'm seething as I stare belligerently at her husband, who is captivated by Two Livers, and seems to be making the mistake of trying to keep up with her as she works her way through the fizz. He should have stuck to Zeros.

'Where does she go to school? I'm very worried about Sven. It's so difficult to get your children into good schools in London.'

'No, it's not.' I rub my thumb and forefinger together. I nod in her husband's direction. 'He can fix it. If he doesn't know his way around, just tell him that when he does a school visit, he should put a brown envelope on the headmaster's desk. Be very open about it. It's expected these days. A grand usually does it.' I tap the side of my nose. 'Cash.'

'Really?' She seems shocked.

'Sure. You must have heard stories about the black economy, the difference between official and real GDP, the unexplained purchasing power and lifestyles of certain professions in this country?'

She shakes her head. 'No.'

'Let's call it oiling the wheels. But you have to be careful how you do it. People over here don't like being handed wedges of cash. You have to be discreet. Always use an envelope, especially if it's anyone official.'

'Official?'

'Sure – the police, for example, if they stop you for speeding. Or the local council, if you want to build an extension on the house, or the magistrates' court, if you get snapped by a speed camera and might lose your licence.'

'I had no idea.'

I shrug. 'Like I said, it's discreet. Just be prepared. Some people keep ready made up envelopes with them all the time.'

'Really? Even in Notting Hill?'

'Notting Hill? Is that where you live?'

'Yes. Ras bought a house there when he first came over. Before I joined him.'

I look pointedly at her husband, who is ignoring us and staring with increasingly lecherous eyes at Two Livers. 'A lot of hookers in Notting Hill.'

'I'm sorry?'

'Hookers. Your husband will explain.' In fact there are a lot of hookers everywhere in London, but I like to say this when people start boring me about property prices and how amazingly well they've done by buying when they did.

'Why did you divorce, Mister Hart?'

'Dave. We're all friends here.' It's a very direct question, but the Scandies can be like that. I wonder how to reply. Should I explain that I'm a selfish, shallow, sex mad, untrustworthy, unreliable son of a bitch? Nah. I put on my wistful look, full of sadness and regret. 'There was something missing from our marriage.'

'What was that?'

I could say trust, honesty and openness, but I've been hitting the champagne pretty hard, and can feel myself just sliding over the edge. 'Blow jobs.'

'Blow jobs?!' She half shouts the words, so that we all look at her and the other people in the bar turn to see what's happening. There's a brief silence, close to exquisite, which I break by half slurring, 'Blow jobs. The secret of a happy marriage is to give your husband at least one blow job every week. Unless you'd rather someone else did.'

\*     \*     \*

IT'S HALF-TIME, and Ras Rasmussen is so pissed he can hardly stand. Vlad has got us a table for dinner in the restaurant, so that we avoid the riff-raff picnicking on the lawn, and we're slurping a fine vintage Chablis to accompany our smoked salmon, swaying and slurring and close to the point where we'll either swear undying love or try to kill each other.

Ras lurches forward across the table towards Two Livers, who still seems alarmingly sober, other than a mild sheen of perspiration across the top of her chest, which beautifully sets off her diamond necklace. Some of the stones are subtly coloured, and I've decided they have to be Leviev.

'So I climbed to the top of Kilimanjaro. The view as the sun rose was spectacular. We set off before dawn and when we reached the summit, we felt so proud.' Ras seems to think this is going to impress Two Livers.

'Is that right?'

He nods, assuming she's going to say how brave and strong and manly he must be, truly a worthy successor to the Vikings who rowed across the North Sea in open boats to burn our villages and screw our women.

'But you haven't tried Everest?'

'Everest?'

'The big one – it's more of a climb than a walk. Or K2?'

He shakes his head.

'Mount McKinley?'

He shakes his head again.

'Or how about some of the little European peaks – the Eiger, the Matterhorn, maybe Mont Blanc?'

Same response. She leans towards me and slips her arm into mine in a semi-proprietorial way. I like it when she does this.

'Dave has.'

'Really?' He looks at me, astonished. I say nothing and sip my wine.

'He does free-fall too.'

'Free-fall?'

'He did a jump over the North Pole.'

'The North Pole?'

She nods and I carry on sipping as if she's talking about someone else. A true hero has no use for self-aggrandisement. 'And he goes heli-skiing in Canada. And he's been diving under the ice in the Antarctic. White water rafting in the Amazon. And filming big game in Africa.'

He's looking at me as if I'm some kind of freak.

'Oh, and one other thing...'

'What's that?'

Just as the bell goes to warn us before summoning us back in for the second half, she grins at him. 'He's captain of the British extreme ironing team as well – they get to iron shirts in the most amazing places...'

Pissed as we are, we crack up, while Ras seethes and Vlad tries to keep a straight face.

Christ, she's good.

\*     \*     \*

I'M AT home – alone once more – in my apartment in Whitehall Court, lying on my bed and reflecting. Like most men, most of the time I spend reflecting is devoted to sex.

Sex is a commodity. You can buy it by the yard, just go on-line to an escort agency website, look at the photos, choose your girl, choose the services you want and make the call. So why is sex with Two Livers different?

Partly it's because she's damned good in bed, knows all the moves and loves it. She really is a natural. But the same is true of a lot of other women. Partly it's because we always have a laugh, but if I've had enough to drink and done a couple of lines of coke, I'll be laughing anyway. I'm starting to wonder if it's something else. Is it possible that it's because she sees me as I am, and despite that we still click together? This thought troubles me. If she can see the real Dave Hart – whoever that is – why should I care? And why should I care if she cares? But I clearly do. This troubles me even more.

Have you ever wondered to what extent we live our

lives through others' perception of us? Labels are meant to describe us, but the fact of having had a label applied can actually define you, changing you from what you really were to what people think you are. Have a medal, now you're officially brave, and what happens – you start to act brave.

I'm a villain. That's my label, I chose it myself and I like it just fine. At times people think I'm controversial, but who cares? Who wants to be uncontroversial? There are enough of those already. Between respecting people's human fucking rights, health and fucking safety, and political fucking correctness, we're turning this country into Bland Land. Somebody has to be Doctor Evil, so why not me? Besides, the villains always get the best parts.

I just wish I didn't keep thinking about Two Livers...

\*     \*     \*

TODAY IS a disaster. I have to be in Madrid for an important presentation to the Development Ministry on New Start for Africa – we're going round all the EU nations, but the Spanish are the most important, because they currently hold the EU Presidency – and the unions representing airline ground staff have decided to go slow.

'Going slow' is an interesting concept for people who never seem to go fast. People who work in the City may not always be the best examples of moral virtue, but they are bright, sharp and work damned hard – otherwise they don't work in the City for very long, if they ever get there in the first place. The problem with working in the City is that it spoils you for the rest of the world outside the Square Mile, where many people are slow, stupid and lazy.

As a result of the industrial action there's mounting chaos in the skies over Britain, and all the small airports are closed, including Biggin Hill, where the Grossbank jets are based. There are no vacant slots available at other airports, so I have no choice but to fly commercial, taking my chances with the great unwashed on public transport.

Naturally I asked Maria to book an entire aircraft for myself and Rory, who is accompanying me to carry my bags. But with hundreds of flights cancelled and thousands of irate passengers desperate not to miss their vacations, democracy prevails and I have to line up with everyone else, which is appalling.

They say the secret of happiness is low expectations. At least that's what Rory always used to say to us at Bartons just before bonus time. But at British airports expectations have to be below rock bottom, and even that is probably way too high.

The first trauma I have to suffer is the indignity of airport security. I'm convinced airport security is a job creation scheme for the terminally stupid and surly. Great lines of us stand around waiting to be processed, while one half of the airline security staff watch the other half watching us line up waiting to be processed. At any moment you sense that someone might do some work, but no, these people are highly trained, and are probably psychologically profiling us to determine which of us will be first to go stark raving mad with frustration.

When it's eventually my turn, I take my shoes and belt off and place my bag on the conveyor belt to be screened. I can't help thinking the Al Qaeda terrorists must be rolling around the floors of their caves in

Afghanistan laughing at the sight of thousands of us meekly lining up like this. Airport security must cost more and cause more delay to the economy than any number of terrorist attacks.

But it does at least keep bad people off the streets, like the obese lesbian working the x-ray machine, who spots my nail-clippers in my wash bag and triumphantly takes me aside.

She unpacks everything from my overnight bag and lays it out for the masses to gawp at. Luckily I'm prepared, and stand proudly beside my change of Calvin Klein underwear, custom-made bespoke shirt from Dege and Skinner of Savile Row, wash bag and grooming kit from Penhaligons, and family-size box of Durex, while the Lumpenproletariat file past, the Ugly Brothers and the Scary Sisters, all making the most of the chance to see what underpants I wear.

It's the grooming kit she homes in on, eagerly seeking out and finding the deadly Ninja fighting nail-clippers that I might have used to storm the flight deck. I agree to surrender them, and she joyfully drops them into a large transparent plastic display cylinder full of similar items, which airport security seem to think will reassure us that they are doing a really great job.

As I repack my bag, I smile and thank her for her contribution towards winning the war on terror.

*       *       *

IT GETS worse.

We are meant to be flying British Atlantic, and go to their so-called Business Class lounge, which is full of travelling salesmen, lower level bankers, management consultants and assorted riff-raff. There are no spare seats, and the bar is running dry.

While Rory queues to fetch me a gin and tonic, I push my way through the crowd to the ogre on the reception desk.

'I'm flying on the 13.15 to Madrid. Can you tell me if it's on time?'

The ogre is theoretically female, probably early fifties, square-jawed, broad-shouldered and ugly. A couple of centuries ago, someone would have hitched a plough to her. Today she seems to relish the misery all around her.

'Your guess is as good as mine.'

'But do you know anything? Have you been told anything?'

'If I had, I'd tell you.' She looks pointedly at the next person, who has a similar question and gets a similar response. I spot another airline employee, a very camp man in his late twenties with a pencil moustache, scurrying around with a sheaf of papers, looking busy and important, but as far as I can tell not actually doing anything.

'Excuse me, I'm meant to be on the 13.15 to Madrid. Do you know if it's on time?'

'I'm sorry, sir, we only know what we're told. You'll have to ask at the desk.'

'The desk don't know anything.'

'Then neither do I, sir. I'm terribly sorry.'

Terribly sorry my arse. I get out my Frequent Flyer Card and use my mobile to call the Gold Card enquiry line. After irradiating my brain for ten minutes, and having still only reached position number seventeen in the queue, I give up and get Rory to call, while I sip my gin and tonic. Even that's lukewarm – they've run out of ice.

This is when the ogre on the desk joyfully announces a series of flight delays. The 13.15 is now the 15.15, and she'll give us more information when she has it. That means I may well miss my meeting, but it isn't her problem. In fact it isn't anyone's problem, except mine. So many people are involved in this chain of irresponsibility, that no one is actually accountable.

We're prisoners. We've checked in, we're through passport control and airport security, and now we're theirs. Hundreds of us. They can abuse us horribly. They can keep us here for hours, feeding us misinformation, supplying gin and tonics without ice cubes, while our business deals crash and burn, and no one is to blame. Of course none of this is necessary, they could do it properly, but as long as we accept it with passive, sheep-like apathy, it's all we'll get.

In the so-called business lounge, I look around at the crowd, at the simperingly ineffectual wimp still wandering about looking important with his sheaf of papers, Rory who still has his mobile tucked under his chin, holding for the Gold Card enquiry line, and I decide that Something Must Be Done.

Since no one else seems capable of doing anything, it had better be me. I'm going to nail these motherfuckers.

I call Paul Ryan. British Atlantic have several billion dollars of debt outstanding. A couple of years ago they borrowed enormous sums in the international markets, issuing bonds to pay for new aircraft and facilities and to invest in new routes, none of which they could manage, because they clearly don't know their arse from their elbow.

Their debt is trading at a discount to issue price, and potential predators have been circling, with a view to buying it, forcing the company to repay it, and when they can't, driving them into bankruptcy.

That would be a wicked plan, because once a company like this is in bankruptcy, you can restructure it, laying off workers, selling off assets, and then re-launch it. People like the ogre and the wimp with their great approaches to customer care might not have jobs after a restructuring, and that would be a terrible thing.

'Paul – start buying. Let's go large.'

My next call is to one of the most feared men on Wall Street, Jerry 'Scarface' Scarpone, the managing partner of Drive-By Capital, known in the hedge fund community as 'the Sicilian'. Drive-By are a rare beast – an honest hedge fund, which is to say that they do what they claim to do. They make great returns for their investors by putting their money into anything bad: gaming companies, arms manufacturers, tobacco companies, even rap artists. The Drive-By Vice Fund was up a hundred and twenty-four per cent last year, which has to tell you something.

'Jerry, have you heard anything about a major lawsuit hitting British Atlantic?'

'A lawsuit? No.'

'Between you and me, this could be big. But don't deal in the stock, okay? This is inside information and you're offside.'

'Understood. We won't deal.'

I look up the British Atlantic share price on my Blackberry. Within seconds it's plummeting. That's the great thing about sharing confidential information with hedge funds – it's far more efficient than issuing public announcements to the market.

The ogre has a TV screen behind her, currently tuned into a classical music channel, presumably on the principle that calming music might stop us going completely berserk.

'Excuse me, would you mind switching to EuroBizTV?'

She can't think of an immediate reason not to, and since this is the business lounge, she reluctantly changes the channel. A few moments later, she looks up as she hears mention of British Atlantic. A newsreader is describing unexpected share price movements following market rumours.

'British Atlantic stock has fallen five per cent today following rumours of impending legal action against the airline. Market commentators have suggested that they may be implicated in the ongoing fuel surcharge row, or in a broader price-fixing investigation in the United States. Meanwhile their bonds have risen dramatically in price, giving rise to speculation that a hostile consortium might be preparing to take control of the airline and force it into bankruptcy and restructuring.'

This gets her attention. Bankruptcy and restructuring? Of her firm? Isn't it strange how our inability to sympathise with our fellow human beings doesn't extend to ourselves?

My next call, leaning on the counter while she ignores

me in case I require customer care or want to ask a question, is to the Silver Fox. I want to do a live interview from the lounge. If I'm really going to be stuck here until 3.15, I might as well have some fun.

After this I call Ron Monk at Toddlers Group. It takes him half an hour before he's doing a 'down the wire' interview for EuroBizTV. It turns out Toddlers are also buying British Atlantic bonds.

'We feel the top management of British Atlantic have been guilty of the twin evils of arrogance and complacency. The market has moved on, the expectations of the travelling public are that much greater, and an airline like this either needs to slash its prices and cut its costs accordingly, or raise its standards of service.'

'Twin evils' – I like that. It was my line but I don't begrudge him. My mobile rings and it's Paul Ryan, sitting round a conference phone with the Grossbank heads of private equity, corporate finance, and a bunch of lawyers and Team Xerox guys.

'Dave – we've got roughly a billion and a half. We're raising our bid, but others are in there competing with us now – Toddlers Group, Downtown, Drive-By, and some of the prop desks. How far should we go?'

'All the way. Let's push it. I want to drive this airline under.'

The ogre is giving me a strange look. The wimp has wandered over and is chatting to her about the latest news reports. They're concerned. This could be a real-time disaster. Not the minor, every-day disaster of people's business trips and holidays being messed up, meetings cancelled, deals failing, family reunions, weddings or funerals missed, bags going astray, precious personal possessions lost, unnecessary, life-shortening angst, hassle and stress, but a real catastrophe – one that might affect them personally.

My next call – with her eavesdropping – is to Vlad the Impaler. OneSib have hired a new prop trading team and they really need a corporate situation to get their teeth into. We call them the Red Army Trading Team, and they have huge capital to make a splash with.

'Vlad – welcome to the club. We've formed a wolf pack and we're taking down a big, fat, lazy cow.' I stare at the ogre as I say this. 'It's called British Atlantic – your guys will find their bonds are moving and it has a target sign pasted to its backside. Time to get off the bench and play, Vlad.'

'Excuse me, what are you doing?' It's the ogre, only she doesn't look quite so daunting now.

'Just some work stuff.' My phone goes, and it's the Silver Fox. I look at my watch. 'Five minutes? Sure.' I hang up and turn back to the ogre. 'I've been asked to do a live interview for television. Is there somewhere I can go to talk privately?'

This snaps her back into normal unhelpful mode – 'This is the Unhelpful Desk and we'd really like you to fuck off and die'. But she can't exactly say that. 'I'm afraid not. We don't have private facilities for passengers.'

'Okay, no problem, I'll do it from here. But maybe you could make a short announcement to ask people to quieten down? I know they won't like it, but if you wouldn't mind…'

As soon as she realises she has the chance to do

something unpopular and blame it on someone else, she leaps at it.

'Ladies and gentlemen, please could we have some quiet in the lounge?' Her voice booms out over the tannoy, much as it would if she were summoning prisoners back to their cells at the end of their exercise period. 'A gentleman at the desk has been asked to do a live television interview. If we could have some quiet in the lounge, we'd be very grateful.'

The noise does die down, as people stare curiously at me, and right on cue the Silver Fox calls, gives me a few final hints, and then I'm live on EuroBizTV, simultaneously talking from the reception desk while an old library shot of me is on the TV screen and my voice is broadcast to the lounge.

'Dave Hart, chairman of Grossbank, market rumours suggest that you are behind moves to take control of British Atlantic. Can you comment on this?'

'Yes, I can. I'm happy to confirm that Grossbank, working with a consortium of institutional investors, has acquired a sufficiently large holding in British Atlantic's bonds to force a meeting with management and potentially to take control of the airline. We'll be holding talks over the next few days, and there will be further announcements in due course.'

'Mister Hart, what does this mean for passengers and staff?'

'We'll be scrutinising performance very closely. As you probably know, British Atlantic has a poor reputation for service.' A loud murmur of agreement goes up from the crowd. 'Naturally there may be some redundancies, and

I'll be taking a personal interest in much of the detail.' This time a cheer goes up. Someone taps me on the shoulder. It's the wimp, looking very pale and servile, and he's brought me a chair to sit on.

'Mister Hart, are there any areas that might be early candidates for closure?'

'Certainly. The London operations hub is the one we'll be looking at most closely. It's high overhead and low productivity. In fact that's where I am today, because I want to see for myself how they cope with the present industrial action. We'll be deciding early on whether to close British Atlantic's facilities, lay off the staff and share with another airline.' I glance across at the ogre. 'We'll do what we have to do, and I guess there will have to be some pain.'

'Dave Hart, Chairman of Grossbank, thank you.'

The amazing thing is, about three minutes later they announce that the 13.15 to Madrid will be leaving on time.

It arrives, at the other end, ten minutes early.

\*       \*       \*

I'M STAYING at the Hotel Molto Grande in Madrid. There's a sign in my suite saying 24 horas al servicio de nuestros clientes. I don't speak Spanish, but you don't need to in order to understand what they're saying. Twenty-four whores at the service of our clients. I call the concierge to book the lot for a private party in the hotel pool after our meeting, but for some reason I can't get him to understand.

Then the buzzer goes and it's Rory, carrying the

presentations we'll be making to the Ministry. The car is downstairs and it's show time.

The Minister is called Emilio Ramos Ramirez, he's short, energetic and enthusiastic. I like enthusiastic people. It's amazing how far a little energy and enthusiasm can take you, especially if you have as big a smile as the Minister.

'So, Mister Hart – you want to save Africa?'

'No, Your Excellency, not at all.'

'Really? I thought that was your plan.'

'Your Excellency, I want to save Europe.'

'Europe?' He glances at the briefing papers on his desk, probably wondering if this is a different meeting.

'Europe, Your Excellency. New Start for Africa is all about Europe.'

He looks relieved that he is after all in the right meeting, but confused at what I'm saying. 'How will the New Start for Africa save Europe?'

'Your Excellency, imagine the world in twenty years' time. A little hotter, the weather patterns changing, traditional crops failing, and Africa still a basket case. Nothing's changed, except to get a little worse. What happens?'

He shrugs. 'We do what we can, within the constraints that are imposed upon us. Our aid budgets are not limitless.'

'With respect, Your Excellency, you're completely wrong. It doesn't take much beyond what we regard as 'normal' disaster conditions to push much of Sub-Saharan Africa over the edge. A couple of degrees hotter, droughts that last a little longer, and countries which are dirt poor, and torn apart by internal conflict, fall completely apart. Forget sending in a few planeloads of grain. Think about half a billion people getting up and heading north, looking for food and shelter, because they've nowhere else to go. You think we have immigration pressure now – try finding space in Western Europe for a few hundred million new arrivals.'

He looks sceptical, but I press on.

'You think they won't get in? How would we stop them? Try building a wall high enough to keep them out. Even my country, which is an island, has lost control of its borders. If we keep Africa poor, they will come. Help them to prosper and they will have a chance to dig their way out. That's why I say I'm not trying to save Africa, but Europe.'

He's nodding now, rubbing his chin, thinking about what I'm saying. He seems a decent enough individual, which probably just means he has the politician's knack of being plausible.

'So what do you want?'

'Nothing.'

'Nothing?'

'No financial contributions, no soft loans, no government guarantees for dodgy African credits – nothing at all. All I ask is that if key individuals in some of the more difficult regimes agree to open up their countries to investment and development, you don't condemn them, you don't harass them if they want to come to Europe, you just leave them be – for as long as they are co-operating. Some of these guys are not exactly pleasant, and their records are not pretty, but we have to be prepared to draw a line, to allow people to change and progress to be made. So I ask you to do... nothing. On a very selective basis.'

He smiles. 'It will be controversial in some quarters. There are people involved in politics who want to pursue certain individuals as soon as they leave the sanctuary of their own countries. But as a politician I believe that we can succeed in doing... nothing. At least for a time, until we see the results of the Grossbank initiative. Congratulations, Mister Hart – you have come with an achievable request, something that even Brussels might manage.'

The great thing about the Spanish is that they care. As foreigners go, they are definitely on the decent side of the equation. They have a natural human empathy. The proposal for certain blacklisted countries in Africa to be rehabilitated if they institute reform programmes is such an obvious no-brainer, especially when tied to fifty billion euros of Grossbank money, that he becomes so friendly I start to get nervous.

Luckily for me he doesn't ask how much money Grossbank will make out of this whole deal.

\*       \*       \*

RORY HAS decided to resign.

It's not that he doesn't like working for me, or find his role as Deputy Chairman of investment banking at Grossbank stimulating and rewarding. In fact he's become much stronger and fitter and lost a lot of weight since he's been rushing around after me carrying armloads of presentations, when he isn't fetching coffee or running errands. It's just that persecuting him has become a competitive sport between Paul Ryan, Two Livers and me. Normally I'm against bullying, except when I do it myself, but Rory is an exception. He has form. And what goes around, comes around, sometimes by the bucketload. Or, in his case, by the skipload.

Paul scored a great coup early on with Rory's mobile phone. Rory made the mistake of leaving it on his desk and Paul spotted it. It's an open secret that Rory has a mistress, a beautiful Mexican woman called Carla who lives in a house in Belgravia. Paul switched the pre-programmed numbers of Rory's wife and mistress. How wicked is that? So when Rory texted his mistress, letting her know he'd be seeing her on the way home, and giving an idea of exactly what he was looking forward to, he got a surprise.

Two Livers was not to be beaten. She told Rory that I had all the senior executive offices and phones bugged. I've no idea what he might have been saying to people about what a great time he was having at Grossbank, or how rewarding it was to work for me, and I'm sure he wasn't so stupid as to talk to headhunters from the office, but he went very pale and quiet.

The next time I saw him, he seemed to be looking at me particularly searchingly. I smiled knowingly and winked, and as she went past, Two Livers nudged him and whispered, 'Don't be lonely. You're never alone with a microphone...'

I couldn't be left out of the fun, so I decided to raise the stakes. We had an off-site to re-organise our Corporate Finance Division from sector teams specialising in particular industries into country teams focussing on businesses located in particular countries or regions. It was a couple of years since Grossbank had re-organised the country teams into sector teams, so it was time for a New Initiative.

We went to Whitely Manor in Sussex, a five-star country-house spa hotel with a Michelin three-star restaurant, and since this was a purely internal occasion with no clients present, we spared no expense. Members of the Management Committee flew in by helicopter. I wanted to arrive playing the Ride of the Valkyries out of loudspeakers on mine, but the Civil Aviation Authority wouldn't allow it – as if they know jack shit about anything to do with flying.

We spent a couple of hours on the first day re-running presentations and strategy papers from the last re-organisation, only in reverse, then the golfers went off to do their thing, I retired to a private section of the spa with Two Livers, and the rest of the Managing Directors and Senior Vice-Presidents started power drinking in the bar.

We all met up for drinks before dinner, and then indulged in a seven-course tasting menu with specially selected wines. For fifty of us, the weekend was a snip at under a million dollars, and represented great shareholder value. I even gave a morale boosting, motivational speech at the end of dinner, explaining how Grossbank was the top of the food chain, and therefore it was appropriate that we had a three-star chef to cook for us. We all thought it was a big laugh, but very good value and important for bonding and teamwork purposes.

Afterwards we played games in the bar. Some of these were drinking games, which made everyone very drunk. Except for me and Two Livers. We're immune, or at least she is. Naturally everyone wanted to be on our team. No one wanted to be on Rory's team.

Around midnight, with everyone pretty much plastered, we moved on to bar diving. Bar diving involves two rows of people lined up at a right angle to the bar, facing each other and linking hands. One person climbs onto the bar and then dives out into their outstretched hands. They have to catch him.

I went first, knowing the bonus round was not far away, and they caught me. Two Livers had no problem, and neither did Paul Ryan. Then it was Rory's turn. He climbed unsteadily onto the bar, looked out into the outstretched hands, and went for it – and damn, the two lines of people let go of each others' hands, stepped aside, and Rory dived off the bar right onto the floor. Must have been a miscommunication. We all rushed forward to pick him up and dust him off, and I brought him another large Scotch. Luckily he wasn't hurt, and he gulped down the whisky, but then he suddenly started slurring his words and passed out – just like that. Wow. Probably drank too much, although one of the MD's who must have had a colourful past said it looked to him like the effects of Rohypnol or one of the other date rape drugs, though how he could know, and how Rory might have swallowed it, was beyond me.

Anyway, a few of us carried him up to his room, undressed him, and left him in bed to sleep it off. But then something very strange happened. Some rascal slipped back into his room, put a condom on the end of a pencil, parted his butt cheeks, slid the pencil inside, and pulled the pencil back out, leaving the condom half in and half out of Rory's backside – and photographed it.

When he came down to breakfast the next day, looking nervous and distracted, he was strangely silent on the matter. Naturally, copies of the photographs were emailed round the office for weeks afterwards, and some went even further afield, ensuring his worldwide reputation in the industry was enhanced enormously.

And now he's gone. No more Rory. By resigning he leaves millions of pounds of unvested shares behind, which I'll have to re-allocate to some deserving cause. I'm feeling pretty deserving myself actually, after finally driving a stake through my old tormentor's heart.

I'd like to say that I really bore Rory no ill will, that time is a great healer, and I don't bear grudges.

But I'd be lying.

*　　　*　　　*

WE'RE IN Singapore for the IMF conference, a bi-annual jamboree to end all jamborees, when tens of thousands of bankers from all over the world gather together to talk, drink, get laid, talk some more, have another drink, get laid again, swap business cards, and if they're up to it, start the same routine again the following day. Some of us, who have exceptional stamina, keep this up all week.

Although in my case it's no different to the rest of my year.

I'm here to take New Start for Africa into its next phase, and I'm feeling quietly confident. I'm giving a speech at the Plenary session, where a couple of thousand senior bankers from all over the world will hear about the New Start and how we're finally going to turn around what is very nearly the last basket case in our increasingly prosperous world.

I take my place with Two Livers amongst the panellists on the stage, waiting to go to the podium to talk. The

Plenary is to be introduced by the Finance Minister of Thailand. There's a stirring in the audience and a sense of anticipation as three stunning women in traditional Thai costume ascend to the stage.

I nudge Two Livers.

'Wow – who brought the hookers?'

She looks horrified, and when I look up, everyone seems horrified. That's when I see the little red light on the microphone in front of me. Out in the audience a couple of thousand faces are going 'Oh...' Two Livers reaches across and turns off my mike.

'Dave, that's June Patanan, the Thai Finance Minister, and her team.'

'She's the Finance Minister? Then I want to be Prime Minister. What a great country.'

Anyone else would have been embarrassed, but luckily I don't give a shit.

The Minister doesn't seem fazed. She acts as if she didn't hear a word and even smiles sweetly at me as she takes her place by the podium. But maybe in Thailand this is the equivalent of laughing your head off at the barbarian tosser who can't keep his mouth shut.

After her welcoming remarks, it's my turn. The applause is a little muted.

'Your Excellency, Ministers, ladies and gentlemen, for those of you who don't know me, my name is Dave Hart and I'm Chairman of Grossbank.' Staggering, isn't it? Someone like me makes Chairman. But I guess someone has to, and mostly it doesn't matter who gets the top job, because they are all the same. Except me. I'm different. 'Most of you will have heard of the initiative we've launched for Africa. We call it the New Start, and we see it not as a charitable initiative, but as a business project. A soundly run, commercial project from which we hope and expect to profit significantly.' Of course we do. We always do. 'We've been working particularly closely with a selection of high profile figures from the worlds of politics and business in a number of African countries, with a view to opening up markets previously closed by political barriers and internal conflicts. We've earmarked fifty billion euros for investment in Africa, and I'm delighted to say we've been supported in our efforts by a number of governments and international organisations, and by the European Union.' Yeah, yeah – I can see the thought bubbles over their heads. They're bored. So am I. 'But still we must do more. One way in which we've sought to put pressure on regimes in Africa to support change has been through our private banking network. Many controversial figures maintain large sums of money in the private banking system, sheltering it from the scrutiny of organisations such as the G8's Financial Action Task Force. I'm pleased to say that the most respected institutions represented here tonight have no part in such business. Their firms are renowned for honesty, integrity and transparency. I'd particularly like to mention the following.' I look around the audience. 'Luc Sturm, of Banque Bruxelloise, are you here?' A balding, portly Belgian sticks his hand up. The Silver Fox has organised the theatrical aspects of tonight's performance, and a spotlight obligingly shines on Mister Sturm as he reluctantly gets to his feet. He wasn't expecting this. 'Let's hear it for Luc and the team from Banque

Bruxelloise.' Muted applause. Then I do the same with Henri Guillaume, of Banque Privée de Gstaad, Damian Van Damme of Privatbank Schlossberg and eventually the heads of half a dozen others. They are standing awkwardly, thinking how cringe-making this all is, but it's nothing compared to what happens next.

'Ladies and gentlemen, I'm delighted to say that all of these banks, the leading private banking institutions in the world, are joining with Grossbank to make a major push against those individuals who choose to use our legitimate banking services to hide dirty money. 'Say No to Dirty Money' will be a new campaign across the banking system, and those individuals who abuse the system will be subject to forfeiture of funds and closure of accounts.'

This stuns them. It's one thing to make people fill out bullshit forms stating their date and place of birth and their inside leg measurement, getting them to provide a photocopy of their passport and birth certificate and other such nonsense, but quite another actually to do anything to stop dirty money coming into the banking system. Money's money after all – for most of these guys there's no such thing as dirty.

It particularly stuns the individuals standing under the spotlights. They had no idea. And worst of all, as the media carry reports of it around the world, it's going to stun the clients whose dirty money they look after.

'Only those individuals whose countries join in with the New Start programme will be able to apply to secure exemptions, under a financial peace and reconciliation programme to be launched under the auspices of the Spanish Presidency of the EU, on a confidential, government to government basis. I'm sure a lot of people will want to take advantage of that.'

I drone on for a few more minutes, and we have a final round of applause for the firms which have supported the initiative. Privately most of the people in the room are amazed that they would ever sign up to such a thing. So are they, because they didn't.

When we file through for dinner, Damian Van Damme grabs my arm.

'Hart – what did you think you were doing with that stunt? You think you can jump us? Force us to go along with your crackpot scheme?'

I keep a fixed smile on my face, because the press cameras are watching. 'That's up to you, Damian. If you want to disassociate your firm from the initiative, I'm sure you can issue the appropriate press release.'

'Business is business, Hart, and money is money. Our doors are open to all comers.'

I don't like Damian Van Damme. Even by the standards of the private banking world, this guy is the Prince of Darkness. He's short, broad-shouldered and swarthy with bushy eyebrows and a thick moustache that reminds me of Borat or maybe one of the Village People.

'Damian, do you really mean that? What about the really bad guys? Mass murderers? Dictators? Mercenaries and criminals masquerading as businessmen?'

He almost spits his reply. 'Especially the really bad guys. You're a fool, Hart. I've had you checked out. You're just a low-flyer who got lucky.'

He's undoubtedly right. But the same could be said of the heads of most major firms. Anyway, I'm not worried.

Not because I'm thick-skinned, but because I have a terrible short-term memory. By tomorrow, what with the booze and all the drugs I'm taking, I'll probably have forgotten what he said, and next time we meet I'll greet him like a long-lost friend.

But not tonight.

We sit down to dinner. I'm at the top table and Van Damme is halfway down the hall. I catch his eye during the entrée, wink at him and raise my glass in an ironic toast.

That does it. He throws his napkin down and gets up to walk out, leaving the people on either side of him wondering what happened.

I get up too, and as he approaches the exit I intercept him to assure him there should be no hard feelings. He's conscious that people are staring at us, and finally nods and grudgingly offers me his hand. But that isn't enough for me. I really want the world to know there's no bad blood between us. After pumping his hand enthusiastically I embrace him, hugging him tightly and slapping him on the back. In fact I'm so all over him that even the surrounding Euro-trash are embarrassed. Englishmen just don't do this stuff. He eventually prises himself free and heads off to the airport to catch an early flight home, while I resume my seat to finish dinner.

And do you know what? The strangest thing happens. Just as we're getting up to leave at the end of dinner we get word from the airport that Damian Van Damme has been arrested. You won't believe this, but it seems he had a monster-sized sachet of Columbian marching powder in his jacket pocket. Naturally he's claiming it wasn't his and that some bastard must have planted it on him, but then he would, wouldn't he? It's amazing who uses the stuff these days. And in Singapore drug smuggling carries the death penalty.

Now there's a thought.

\*     \*     \*

WHEN SHE has a really massive orgasm, even Two Livers has to stop multi-tasking.

Women are amazing. She came to my suite to go through the next day's programme, found me about to get down to business with a couple of Chinese girls, showed them the door, got undressed and climbed into bed, all the while running through the meeting schedule and background notes on the chairmen and chief executives of the firms I'll be meeting. It was only when I managed to score nine on the Richter scale that she briefly stopped talking.

Our key task now is to get more governmental support. I'm due to attend a reception and dinner for Development ministers of the leading industrialised nations, and I need to roll the dice again. A lesser man would be nervous, but luckily I'm too shallow to be nervous.

And in the meantime, I have the perfect distraction…

\*     \*     \*

NEVER TRUST a banker.

I told Ramos Ramirez that I didn't want money out of any European governments. That was fair enough as banker-speak goes, but like so much of what investment bankers tell their clients, it probably shouldn't be taken at face value.

In reality I want lots of money from European governments, but just haven't told them yet. I like to think of it as a subtle difference of interpretation that we'll work around to in due course.

Others might just say I was lying.

The art of negotiating with clients or other providers of revenues, deal-flow and other key components of the bonus pool, is to let the other side have your own way. It's often said that the best investment bankers don't rape their clients, they seduce them – because that way they can keep on fucking them.

Drinks are being served with the ministers and their senior civil servants along with various bankers, journalists, and assorted flunkies before a smaller group – just the thirty of us – sit down for an intimate dinner followed by speeches.

The British Development minister is here, an early forties, up-and-coming hot shot called Benjamin Hillary. I spot him chatting to some kind of babe, presumably somebody's wife or mistress, who's dressed like a designer Christmas tree with labels in all the right places. I leave them to chat for a few minutes, observing and taking things in until I can see the Minister is bored, looking discreetly over her shoulder for someone to rescue him.

I nearly dive straight in, but a really cute waitress is standing in front of me with a tray of spring rolls. She's Chinese, very deferential, with long black hair, huge eyes and a very trim figure. Definitely a possibility. I glance at the spring rolls.

'May I take one?'

'Yes, of course. I have napkins here. You can use your fingers.'

'Is that right?' I hold her gaze. 'I'm very good with my fingers…'

She smiles and looks away, and I'm about to say something else when I feel a hand on my shoulder. It's Two Livers.

'Dave, don't go off-piste yet. The UK Minister needs rescuing. Grab him while you can.'

Benjamin Hillary does look utterly bored. He's actually backed slowly away from the designer Christmas tree, but she's followed him, and they've gradually worked their way through the crowd until he now has his back literally to the wall. Time the cavalry arrived.

I move through the crowd until I'm standing next to the Christmas tree. When I see her up close, she's not such a babe. She's probably mid-fifties, speaks with a central European accent and has the self-confidence of a Euro-trash aristo – probably an Austrian countess. She looks as if she's had every age-defying form of surgery known to man, and I mentally dismiss her as Mrs Plastic Fantastic. Worse still, she's loud, has too much make-up on and exudes the certainty that she's not only the most attractive and amusing woman at the party, but that all of us want to seduce her. If she were British, a decade or so younger and male, she could be me.

As I move in alongside her I step on her Demi-Monde shoe.

'Ow!' She looks at me accusingly.

'Oh, I'm sorry, I do apologise.'

She's staring at the pointy toe of her five-thousand-pound shoe.

'Are those shoes by Demi-Monde?'

'Yes.' She's not sure whether to be flattered that I noticed, or angry that I may have spoilt one of them.

'Disgraceful.'

'Disgraceful? What do you mean?' She's getting ready for a fight.

I look at Benjamin Hillary. 'Disgraceful that someone should come to an event like this wearing a five thousand pound pair of shoes. No one needs five- thousand-pound shoes. Wear a five-hundred-pound pair and give the rest to charity.'

She looks at me dismissively. 'I do give to charity. Lots in fact, every year.'

'Then give more.'

She looks to the Minister for support, but he's staring into his glass, and she turns on her heel and disappears without saying another word. Finally he looks up from his glass and speaks.

'Mister Hart, that was very rude, but I agree with you.'

How about that? He knows me already. I like this guy.

'Minister, I'm sorry if I pissed you off. But I speak my mind. I don't know any other way.'

He looks at me a little sceptically. He knows I'm a banker. It goes without saying that I know all kinds of ways, and that generally the last thing I do is speak my mind. I speak whatever the client wants to hear.

I start to talk about the New Start programme, but he's there ahead of me.

'Mister Hart, cut the crap. How much will Grossbank make out of New Start?'

'Billions.' I say it with confidence, and strictly speaking it's true. In fact I'm hoping that by getting in early and cherry-picking our investment projects, we'll more than double our money over the next five years. But fifty billion times two, is quite a large number, and I don't want to trouble him with detail. I can see he's a big picture man.

'I assumed so.' He sips his drink slowly, scrutinising me over the rim of his glass.

I feel strangely naked. Normally I like being naked, but this is different. I shrug half-apologetically. 'I'm a banker. Even my dark side has a darker side.'

He nods. 'I know.' More scrutiny. What does he know? What can he know? Maybe some special government department has a file on me and he read it on the plane out. Or maybe I have a pimple on the end of my nose, but just haven't realised it yet. He rubs his chin reflectively. 'But I'm still going to support you.'

Phew. 'Why is that?'

'Because what you're doing is what should be done, only most people aren't prepared to contemplate... what shall we say...? The unusual methodology you sometimes employ.'

Unusual methodology? This is scary. I tend to freak out when people know things about me that I don't know that they know.

'Mister Hart, do you really think everything can be financed by the private sector?'

Time to level with him. He probably knows the answer anyway. 'Not everything, no. Not everything that needs to happen is commercially viable. Some things will always require government money, aid money, contributions from supra-national organisations.'

'So why aren't you asking us?'

'So far no one has a problem with what I'm doing, even if the methods are... unconventional... because I don't have my hand out.'

A dork has appeared beside us and wants to meet the Minister. His badge identifies him as a journalist. He hovers within earshot, waiting to be acknowledged. Where are the Meat Factory when you need them? If only they were here they could throw him out the window. Well, dangle him upside down anyway.

The Minister turns to the journalist and shakes hands, but just before he starts talking to him, he turns back to me briefly. 'Be bold, Mister Hart. You might get a surprise.'

He wanders off with the journo. I like the guy. He strikes me as really smart. As a politician he actually chooses to do long hours of tedious work, mixing with second-rate people, for piss poor money, just so he can make a difference.

Maybe he's not so smart after all.

\*     \*     \*

'FAILURE ISN'T falling down. Failure is not getting up again.'

Dinner is over and I'm addressing the ministers and senior officials in a large private dining room.

'In Africa people are used to falling down. They fall down every time there's a drought, or disease makes their crops fail, or warlords or bandits come and steal their food and burn their homes. But they keep on getting up. They keep on getting up, even when we don't lend a hand. Well, Grossbank is lending more than a hand. We're putting our money where our mouth is, and have committed fifty billion euros.'

I glance across at Benjamin Hillary, who is sitting at the end of the table next to Ramos Ramirez. Fuck it, time to sound the bugles and charge. I put down my notes, and across the table from me Two Livers does one of her 'Oh Christ, he's going off message' looks.

'Fifty billion doesn't sound much if you say it quickly. But it's more than I could spend in a weekend.' This gets a few polite smiles. Even I couldn't get through that much, though it would be fun trying. 'But it will achieve a huge amount. So far seven countries have started working with Grossbank on New Start investment projects. All of these countries have had, let's just say, a controversial past. But we've approached them at the highest level...' Which is to say at the level of their leaders' wallets. '...And have been able to open doors and markets. But private money can't do everything. We're accountable to shareholders, we might take risks, but we have to show a return. Some projects simply can't show the returns we need, like basic infrastructure in rural areas without natural resource potential. But these projects matter too, and taken together alongside the New Start projects the cumulative impact can be huge.' Which is to say that Grossbank needs these countries to be stable, but won't pick up the tab itself. 'We can get whole regions out of the mire and permanently standing on their own feet. All we need is to decide to do it. Because real people's real lives are at stake. Millions of them. I believe it would be a crime not to do something when we can. If we simply turn aside, then it should be on all of our consciences. Thank you.'

When I sit down, my eyes are shining as if I'm fighting back the tears and I have a lump in my throat. They can feel the emotion. At times like this I feel like a method actor, and sincerity is one of my specialities. Christ, I'm good.

Ben Hillary's been waiting for this. He turns to Ramos Ramirez, who is technically our host tonight.

'With your permission, Emilio, I'd like to pick up on Mister Hart's last comments.' Ramos Ramirez nods his consent, and Hillary looks around the table at his counterparts from other nations.

'We're often criticised for saying a lot but doing little.' Lots of wise nodding round the table. It's true. The wealthy nations don't get a great press, mostly because they don't deserve one. 'The developed world makes pledges, grabs a few headlines, then quietly walks away without delivering.' More wise nodding. A lot of these guys like it that way. 'New Start gives us a real opportunity to break the mould. Once and for all.' Now they're looking alarmed. This wasn't covered in the pre-IMF talks where their officials agreed in advance what the Ministers would agree. 'As a group, we should commit here and now, this evening, to match Grossbank's contribution, euro for euro, as the funds are committed, and over whatever time period is involved. Fifty billion euros. With effect from today.' Ah, they can see his game now. The devil, as they say, is in the detail. The funds will only go in as Grossbank puts the money in. That could take years, and might never happen. It's another pledge, another vague agreement to agree, or in political speak a decisive, strategic determination to talk about talks.

Smiles all round and heads nod. This really will be a surprise. People will see that the developed world doesn't just spend its time talking about itself at these great gatherings. We find time for headline grabbing gimmicks as well.

Ramos Ramirez is delighted. This will be an initiative of the Spanish Presidency. It's so vague and non-binding that none of them needs to clear it with their own capitals. One after another they fall into line, pledging their support. In under fifteen minutes it's a done deal. Even the French are happy to agree.

Ramos Ramirez calls the press in and they hold an impromptu briefing. The hacks scribble away, cynically dismissing it all as another PR stunt, until I clear my throat and turn to Ramos Ramirez.

'Your Excellency, with your permission, may I?'

He's all smiles and bonhomie. 'Of course, Mister Hart.'

He really ought to know better. 'Ladies and gentlemen, there is one further detail that His Excellency omitted to mention.' He suddenly looks nervous. Too late, pal. 'The funds pledged tonight will be taken in by Grossbank and held in a special high interest account, at no charge to the nations involved, until they are drawn down. Within ninety days. This is a real commitment.'

The hacks are amazed. The Ministers even more so. Real? No one talked about real. And where did ninety days come from? Even as I say the words, you can see a few political careers going into a nose dive when they get home and have to account for making commitments without authorisation or consultation, especially ones where real money gets spent.

Benjamin Hillary looks across at me. I guessed he'd do this, taking a leaf out of my book to jump his oppos'. What he didn't know is that I'd jump the jumper. I smile at him. Never trust a banker, pal.

But then he smiles back and he really looks delighted. Shit. Who's the cat and who's the mouse here? They say he's a conviction politician, and very bright, and then it dawns on me. He wanted this to happen, and he knew I'd jump him. He jumped the jumper who was jumping him. Christ, he's good. If he ever wants a job at Grossbank, he can have any role he wants.

Except mine.

*     *     *

SUCCESS IS relative. Mobilising a hundred billion for the worst basket cases in Africa, getting their leaders to agree to phased, peaceful regime change, helping tens of millions of people to achieve a better life – well, at least a more material one – and all the while earning monster bonuses, having sex with some of the most beautiful women in the world, getting pissed and doing drugs night after night probably sounds pretty good to most people.

But as it works, so the emptiness sets in again.

I hate those 'What's it all for?' moments that creep up on you in the early hours of the morning, when the girls are asleep and you're lying awake, staring at the ceiling. I don't really think it's for anything at all. It just is. Which leaves a gaping hole inside me that I fill with drugs and booze and momentary pleasures.

Except maybe Two Livers. Maybe she's different.

Maybe she's the one. She's brighter, harder working, far more talented than I could ever be.

We're going on a tour of African capitals together. Just the two of us in a smoker for a week, visiting some of the places that she thinks might change the way I view the world.

This afternoon I was so bored I agreed to chair the Management Committee – third time this year – and she sent me a text message: 'OUCH!'

We were just talking about rationalising the branch network in Germany, imposing compulsory redundancies on one in ten of the workforce, and I creased up, which left everyone rather puzzled. 'OUCH!' is code for 'I'm at the beauticians having a waxing, and I've just had a Brazilian'. Now that's commitment.

While the Management Committee drone on about job cuts, all the while casting nervous glances towards the madman at the head of the table, I sit there grinning, trying to work out what turns me on more – the thought of Two Livers' almost hairless pussy, or the idea of watching some eastern European beautician – Voluptuous Vesi from Bucharest – carrying out the waxing.

I wonder if I could pay to watch.

*　　*　　*

THE REAL reason I went to the Management Committee was an item that came up under the HR report. Apparently we have a sexual harassment problem with a female employee. No, it isn't what you're thinking. Caroline Connor has changed. The six-foot-one-inch librarian that I wanted to connect with all the tall guys in the firm has become a man-eater. It worked. She's changed her hairstyle, swapped the glasses for contacts, wears miniskirts up to her armpits and is working her way steadily through all the tall, single, good-looking men in the firm. They tell me she rides to work on a Harley Davidson and even has a tattoo.

The problem is that good-looking, well built, six-foot-three-inch tall, high-achieving men are psychologically ill-equipped to be prey rather than predators. A couple have left, while others – get this – have complained. Officially. Can you believe that?

HR want to initiate a disciplinary procedure. I agree with them. Fire the fuckers. What's wrong with them? But then the HR people start to give me all this political correctness shit about Caroline Connor, and it's her they want to fire. I feel like I've nodded off and woken up in a short story by Kafka. An attractive woman keeps pestering you to have sex with her, takes you to bed and exhausts you, night after night, and you think it's a problem?

I say, hell no, she's one of the most original thinkers in the firm and I won't lose her. If the guys have a problem with one of my best people, then as far as I'm concerned they're the problem. We should treat them no differently than anyone else who complains about being harassed by one of our key people – either we find a reason to fire them or we invent one, and if we really can't do that, we pay them off. This is not the kindergarten – we're talking investment banking in the twenty-first century. I'm willing to risk a class action suit against the firm on behalf of all the tall, handsome men in the industry, providing it means I get to keep my Amazon. Even if she is too tall for me.

I look at the HR people. 'Who are we?'

'Grossbank.' They say it in a half-hearted, 'we don't really get this' tone.

'And?'

'Grossbank rocks.'

Enough said.

*       *       *

AFRICA IS different. All the clichés in the world are inadequate when it comes to the dark Continent, and Two Livers was right. Dirt poor people with mile wide smiles, amazing sunsets, vast distances, a sense of actually being alive. For a week I've been off the drugs and still felt the buzz. It's been a great trip, and I've never felt as close to another human being as I do now to Two Livers.

I'm about to indulge in a glass of my drug of choice in Africa, alcohol, in this case vintage Bollinger, in the back of Air Force One, as I call my favourite Grossbank smoker.

I'm with Two Livers and we're celebrating the signing of a New Start programme for Lubumbashi, having stayed in a hotel so primitive that it had no air conditioning, only sporadic running water, and food so dire that we were warned by Ralph Jones, 'If it's not cooked, or you can't peel it, leave it on the plate.' I even took the radical step of skipping ice cubes in my gin and tonic, so great was my fear of infection.

So we visited the markets, went to a special concert given by schoolchildren as guests of honour, and took a river trip to spot crocodiles and hippos, which we named in honour of colleagues in London.

We took a whole day out of our programme and went

to the beach and swam in the sea, while our hosts freaked out. The waters around here are shark-infested, and they didn't want to lose us before we signed. We were relaxed. Investment bankers never get taken by sharks. There is such a thing as professional respect.

Oh, and we had amazing sex, including a great scene in the surf, which should have been filmed as a movie classic.

But now we've signed, and General Van Smit has told us how the government forces have cleared out their old friends the warlords, who are mighty pissed off. He reckons they've sworn undying hatred of Grossbank and of me personally, and tells me to watch out.

So you can imagine how relieved I am when I'm sitting in the back of the plane with Two Livers, climbing rapidly to cruising altitude and leaving anger, greed and hostility behind – so we can get back to the everyday anger, greed and hostility of ordinary investment banking.

Everyday life, even as an investment banker, is going to be very boring after what we've been doing. We now have eleven countries signed up to New Start programmes. We've committed thirty of our fifty billions, and the EU are committed to matching amounts. We really are making a difference. And the impact on the bonus pool is going to be astronomical. It definitely hasn't been boring.

Two Livers and I lean forward and clink glasses.

'Success.'

She smiles. 'And the future.'

I wonder what she means. Part of me hardly dares to speculate. Clothes, jewellery, fast cars, private jets? Or something else?

'Hey, I couldn't have done this without you, you know.'

'I know.' She speaks with a beautifully deep, sexy voice. 'In fact, you couldn't have done jack shit without me. Or Paul. Or half a dozen other people. But none of it would have happened without you. You really are different, you know. In fact...'

There's a sudden flash and a bang outside the cabin window, and the plane lurches to one side, emptying our glasses and tipping up the ice bucket, sending the champagne bottle rolling along the floor.

'Christ, what was that?'

The pilots are both at the controls, the door shut behind them for privacy, but one of them shouts over the intercom, 'Missile! Someone's fired a missile at us.'

We stare at each other. This was definitely not meant to happen. The plane is vibrating, shaking and shuddering like it's about to fall apart. We hear the pilot's voice again. 'Mayday, mayday, mayday, this is Gulfstream Golf Bravo seven niner, we have been struck by a missile and are losing height, estimated two minutes to impact, our position is...'

Two Livers stares at me, horrified. 'Christ – we're going down.'

'Going down? Then...' I fumble to undo my seatbelt. Opposite me, she unbuckles hers, throws herself on top of me, rips my shirt open and starts undoing my belt. 'Two minutes...'

That's when I see another flash out of the corner of my eye, there's a much louder bang and a sudden, howling rush of air.

Damn!

# WHERE EGOS DARE
by David Charters
*from Elliott & Thompson*

I THINK I'm going mad.

I know I can't be dead. I know because it's hot as hell, and that simply does not compute. How could I have died and gone to hell? It's impossible. Hell is for other people. In fact hell *is* other people. It's certainly not for me.

There's a hot wind blowing over me like a giant hair dryer. I'm lying on my back, being dragged across a surface that alternates between smooth and rough, and my body is aching. The whole of my right side is hurting, as if my ribs are broken. Maybe they are. The sun – at least, I suppose it's the sun – is burning my face and I'm keeping my eyes tightly closed.

But at least I can't be dead. That's important. Because where would the world be without me?

My mouth is parched and my lips feel painful and cracked. I slide and lurch forward a few more yards. Whatever it is I'm lying on is being pulled, slowly, across the ground. Somewhere nearby I hear a soft sigh that's feminine, wonderful, a weak-strong moan of someone exhausted but determined.

That's when the memories come back.

I was flying home to London, from a business trip to Africa. I was in a private jet – a Gulfstream 5, my personal favourite, about to sip champagne and toast success – when there was an explosion. I recall the pilot's voice frantically calling in a Mayday, then another loud bang and everything is hazy.

Until now. Now the memories are flooding back.

I'm Dave Hart.

Knowing my name is important, at least it is for me. With that comes a whole avalanche of other memories. I'm a banker. At the tender age of forty, I became Chairman of the Erste Frankfurter Grossbank, one of the largest financial institutions in the world, and took the whole giant organisation into overdrive. I've achieved things, made things happen, financed the unfinanceable, poured money into projects in Africa that no one would touch, changed the world. I've done things in the world of business that no other human being ever has. And some that no other human being would ever want to. Either way, I'm a finance rock star.

I'd been visiting Lubumbashi, a godforsaken dump of a place where Grossbank's New Start Plan for Africa – an investment plan to acquire assets and develop them in return for introducing proper governance and democratic institutions – was re-shaping a nation. I was re-shaping a nation. That sort of thing appeals to me. I like changing things, upsetting people, pissing them off. And I like to think big. If you're going to bother to think, it's the only way to go. Only this time someone got really pissed off. Pissed off enough to fire a rocket up the arse of my G5.

There was someone with me. Someone beautiful. An intelligent blonde. Yes, really. Funny too and sexy as hell. And she could drink.

Two Livers.

Laura 'Two Livers' MacKay, my head of corporates at Grossbank, my right hand woman, key business winner, planner, strategist, possessor of a brain the size of a planet and a body to die for, was with me when the plane crashed.

Two Livers is different from any woman I've ever known, and yes, I've known a few. When God made blondes, I truly believe he took all of their brains and gave them to this one woman. In my rare moments of lucidity I'll admit – privately – that most of my success I owe to her.

She was also my lover.

'Aaaaaagh…' A woman's voice. Weaker now. I'm not being pulled forward any more. My hand slips from the side of what I guess is a makeshift stretcher and touches hot sand. Desert sand. I've been pulled across the desert. By her. I feel the end of the stretcher slowly being lowered to the ground, gently, so that I'm resting on the desert sand, hot through the canvas.

Damn. I guess it means I have to get up.

I open one eye cautiously. No need to worry. I can see her kneeling a few yards from me, her head slumped forward, her beautiful blonde hair falling forward over her face, the tattered remains of what was once a beautiful Chanel dress hanging loosely over her perfect body. She's barefoot. Walking barefoot on the hot desert sand. Like a slave girl. The fantasy part of my brain whirrs into action.

It's like a scene from a movie. If I wasn't in so much pain I'd think about jumping her right now. Although having sex on a dune is always a bad idea. Sand gets in all the wrong places.

My own clothes are just as badly torn, my shirt hanging in shreds around me. I ease myself up painfully onto one elbow and watch as she slowly rolls forward until her head touches the sand. She's instinctively curled into a tight ball, exhausted, vulnerable, her last reserves gone.

Bugger. Now I'll have to get up and start walking.

I pull myself over and slowly stand up. I've certainly cracked several ribs, and I feel weak and slightly dizzy. I'd kill for a drink. In fact several, plus a decent meal and maybe a sharp, reviving line of white powder. But at least I'm alive. The sun is unreasonably hot, and I stare in wonder at the tracks left in the sand, extending far away into the distance. She's been pulling me for miles, for hours, through the heat of the desert, on a makeshift stretcher made out of two twisted metal poles and a length of canvas. Why would an investment banker do that? Would any banker truly rescue his boss, if he had the choice not to and no-one would ever find out? How much more would Two Livers stand to make each year without me top-slicing the bonus pool?

I walk over to her and crouch down beside her, gently stroking her hair. She's gone, dead to the world. I put my hands under her shoulders and struggle to pull her onto the stretcher. It's an effort, but once she's there I pick up the end and prepare to walk forwards, dragging her in the same direction she was pulling me.

Damn, it's hard. She may be delightfully slim, but to

me in this heat she feels heavy. Forget heroics. This is no
fun at all. After a couple of paces I ease her back onto the
ground. I don't know if I'm exhausted or lazy, but there's
no way I'm dragging her across the desert. I stare into the
distance. It looks the same in each direction, just miles of
undulating dunes.

I analyse things the way that only a senior
investment banker can. This is a truly desperate, life
threatening situation. It's not like the ordinary,
everyday problems I have to endure in London, like
not getting my favourite table for an early evening
martini at Duke's Hotel, or getting stuck in traffic on
my way to see Fluffy and Thumper from the Pussy Cat
Club for a private performance. I could actually die. *I
could really fucking die!*

I look at Two Livers, exhausted and unconscious from
her ordeal. Damn. Two of us certainly won't make it, at
least with me pulling. For both our sakes I need to leave her
here – obviously after first checking she's comfortable – and
then head off by myself to fetch help. I know I'm fond of
her and all that, but it's in both our interests. Honestly. In
fact it's because I care for her that I have to leave her now.
I'm doing this for her.

Phew, that was easy.

Having taken my decision, I start to head off by myself,
but I've only gone a few paces when I seem to hear a
strange sound. Perhaps I'm imagining it, but I'd swear I
can hear a tacka-tacka-tacka noise. Maybe it's just in my
head. Fuck it. Must be the heat. Or the drugs. What have
I been using lately? Not much, travelling in Africa. In fact
I've been remarkably clean. I shake my head to clear it

and prepare to head off once more in search of salvation –
for us both, of course.

That's when the helicopter appears over the nearest
ridge of sand.

Also by
**DAVID CHARTERS**

## AT BONUS TIME, NO ONE CAN HEAR YOU SCREAM

Meet Dave Hart. Dave is worried. He's an investment banker and it's not long until 'B' day, the most important day of the year. He's thinking what he would do with a million pounds. But we all know a million just isn't what it used to be...

## TRUST ME, I'M A BANKER

Dave Hart is standing in the office of his boss on bonus day, with a machete. It's not usual practice on bonus day, but then Dave is not your usual investment banker. Something the owners of German sleeping giant 'Grossbank' seem to have noticed.

## NO TEARS: TALES FROM THE SQUARE MILE

The original collection of short stories from David Charters lifts the veil on the dark heart of the City. Greed, ambition, ego and cunning conspire to triumph in this dog eat dog world, but often with startling twists. If you think you know how it all works in the Square Mile, *No Tears* will have you thinking again.